You Are Not Needed Now

ALSO BY ANNETTE LAPOINTE

Stolen (Novel)

Whitetail Shooting Gallery (Novel)

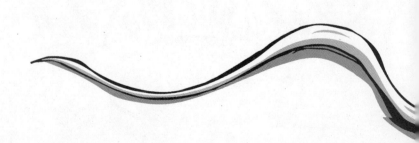

You Are Not

Stories by
Annette Lapointe

Needed Now

Anvil Press Publishers Inc.
P.O. Box 3008, Main Post Office
Vancouver, B.C. V6B 3X5 CANADA
www.anvilpress.com

Library and Archives Canada Cataloguing in Publication

Lapointe, Annette, 1978-
[Short stories. Selections]
     You are not needed now : (stories) / Annette Lapointe.

Short stories.
ISBN 978-1-77214-093-4 (softcover)

     I. Title.

PS8623.A728A6 2017   C813'.6   C2017-903383-2

Printed and bound in Canada
Cover design by Rayola Graphic
Cover illustration by William Zach
Interior by HeimatHouse
Represented in Canada by Publishers Group Canada
Distributed by Raincoast Books

The publisher gratefully acknowledges the financial assistance of the Canada Council for the Arts, the Canada Book Fund, and the Province of British Columbia through the B.C. Arts Council and the Book Publishing Tax Credit.

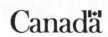

For John

ACKNOWLEDGMENTS

"Scatterheart" originally appeared in *Grain*.

"Clean Streets Are Everyone's Responsibility" originally
appeared in *The Danforth Review*.

"You Are Not Needed Now" originally appeared
in *Prairie Fire*.

CONTENTS

The Waiting List
for Martyrs

I WOKE UP BECAUSE SHE WAS IN THE LIVING ROOM, crying. For a minute, I thought I'd dozed off in the ladies' room at work. I do that, sometimes. We have an old-fashioned fainting couch behind a divider, and if I haven't had enough sleep I'll lie down there for a bit during lunch. Occasionally, someone assumes there's no one in there and turns off the light and I sleep for hours. They think I've gone home. Then the light comes on again and someone locks herself into a stall. Sits there and cries.

I don't know that men's rooms have the same problem with crying. Maybe they do.

When that happens, I try to leave as discreetly as I can. Pretend I didn't hear anything. No one is crying. No one is here.

I checked myself: no bra, nightie. The surface under me was the tangle of my bed. I wasn't at work. The neighbour cried sometimes, but he was a man, and he sounded different.

When I came out to my living room, carrying my phone in case I needed to call the police, she was curled up in one corner of the couch, watching TV. A lady of about seventy, in blue sweatpants and a pink T-shirt. No bra on her, either. She'd made herself a cup of coffee.

She was crying. *Weeping.* Based on the heap of used tissues lurking on the floor, she'd been crying for ages. It didn't interrupt her viewing. While I watched, she switched channels again.

I said, "Who *are* you?"

"Oh," she said. "I'm so sorry." She disappeared. She left behind the Kleenex.

⇐ ⇐ ⇐

When I was in grade eight, we had a student teacher in French. If I think hard about it, I can picture her — a whirl of curly auburn hair, probably coloured, but I wasn't used to women colouring their hair other than blonde, so I presumed it was real. That's all I have left. She was pretty, for whatever that's worth. I think she was pretty. She was young, at least.

I only remember her because she asked my class for something that no experienced teacher would have: she asked us to each do a presentation of our family trees. It must have been part of a vocabulary lesson:

la mere	*the mother*
le père	*the father*
la soeur	*the sister*
le frère	*the brother*
le grande-père	*the grandfather*
la grande-mère	*the grandmother*
la tante	*the aunt*
l'oncle	*the uncle*
le cousin/la cousine	*the cousin*

We must have been just coming to the end of the period where it was polite to ask about that sort of thing. By the time I was old enough to try my hand at teaching, we knew better. We avoided all those questions: When were your parents married? What does your father do? How many sisters and brothers do you have? I became a teenager right at the end of the world in which you could expect a definite answer.

She wasn't prepared for our answers. The first few presentations took an hour or so each. After that, she just collected the work on paper. I remember I was angry that she didn't call on me to present. I'd done real work on it. I'd gone to our neglected family bible (illustrated by Dali, dusty, but at some point my father had carefully inked in every family member he could remember). I'd gone to my then-still-living grandparents. I'd found two uncles were doing genealogical research.

I made a chart. We didn't have a computer at home, then, so there wasn't fan-fold paper. Instead, I taped sheet after sheet together, making careful hinges, so that the whole map could fold down into a booklet. Everyone was on it. I looked up the French words for *second-cousin* and *great uncle* in the dictionary!

Like, I suspect, many of my classmates, I came to the French teacher with a list of relationships the dictionary didn't cover, and she sighed, and carefully wrote each word out for me.

The 1991 report, *Ma famille, par April C.*, became a family classic. I'd recorded 183 relatives.

€ € €

This is how a woman becomes in charge of things. She expresses an interest in a period before she thinks it matters. During the next two and a half decades, it becomes familial knowledge that April is interested in the family tree.

I received my first pack of handwritten notes in 1993. They'd been exhumed from a cardboard box of my great-grandfather's papers. The box was in my great-aunt's closet when she moved into a nursing home in Ontario.

Some of it was family records. They were mixed in with receipts from the 1970s and programs from funerals for people I'd never heard of and who didn't appear in the records anywhere. My mother looked at the papers and told me, "Those might be important. Hang on to them."

By the time my parents retired, they were holding more than a dozen plastic tubs of mixed documents for me. Unlike my parents, I didn't have a barn to put them in, but I took them. They filled the second bedroom of my apartment for years. Finally, I paid someone I found on the Internet to scan them all. Nice kid from the university where I don't teach anymore. Teaching's a temporary gig for all but the dedicated few; for the rest of us, there's administration. I manage personnel files for the pension managers.

After she'd scanned it all for me and put the documents on a set of CDs, I asked her to help me load the boxes into my car. "Where are you taking them?"

"There's a recycling centre behind the Safeway."

"What? No way. You should give those to the archives. For the public record, you know?"

The university archives were happy to take the records. Their next available intake slot was six years away.

I came home late from a pub night with the girls from accounting and there was a dusty man in a bathrobe pecking at a ghostly typewriter in my spare bedroom. He'd set it up on the futon, and sat cross-legged. Under the bathrobe, he wasn't wearing anything.

I said, "Can I, I don't know, *get* you anything?"

"I'm fine, sweetheart. You go on to bed."

I phoned my mother. She and my dad had moved into a condo in an adults-only, over-fifty-five complex in south Saskatoon. It had a twice-weekly shuttle to one of the new big-box centres that seem to have replaced malls. My parents liked the shuttle. They liked buses, period. All summer, they took bus tours to places of historic interest in northern Saskatchewan. During the winter, my dad sorted the pictures on his computer and made slideshows that he emailed to everyone in the family.

My mom put them on Facebook, which seems to satisfy everyone involved.

I said, "Do you have somewhere I can put all these papers?"

"We moved, remember?"

"I know."

"I think your place is bigger than ours."

"I know."

"If you don't want them," my mother said, reasonably, "throw them away."

❦ ❦ ❦

A Facebook survey of my extended family (eighty-two charted family members active online) indicated that several cousins wanted to have a look through the papers before I threw them away. One or two asked if I wanted anything from a garage clear-out:

china cabinet (Eaton's catalogue, circa 1932)

blue portable typewriter, ribbon needed

a box of glass inkwells

selected jewellery

two vintage evening bags, age uncertain

medal from a tennis tournament, 1948

I said, "Have a garage sale. Hipsters love that stuff."

The woman in the pink T-shirt dropped a Kleenex onto my desk. It seeped wetly. She said, "I think that medal's mine."

"Do you want it?"

"Yes, please, dear."

By that time, I'd logged six regular visitors. I didn't know any of them by their first names. I needed pictures so I could present them to my mother, but I wasn't sure of the etiquette of photographing ghosts. Would my phone's camera work? If I needed something more complex, would any of the 1960s camera gear in the box in my front closet do a better job?

My cousin sent the medal, with a small note indicating that she wouldn't mind being reimbursed for the cost of postage. I left the medal out on the table for a few nights, but no one showed up for it. I threw the note in with my recycling.

The woman in the pink T-shirt woke me up, crouching beside the bed. Her fingers clutched the note about the cost of postage. It appeared to have coffee grounds on it, and something like egg. "I'm so sorry, dear. I didn't realize how much it was going to cost. I'll see what I have in my purse."

I said, "I'm pretty sure I didn't get your purse."

She didn't take the medal. I put it in the camera box. She stood on the other side of the shower curtain the next morning and said, "Those cameras aren't mine."

I packed the box into my car and took it to work. On the way home, I found a brand new self-storage place just off Preston. "How much?"

The first three months were on special for only thirty dollars. Later, it would cost more. More than I could afford. But three months seemed like a long time. In three months I could find a cousin to take the boxes in. I could emigrate. While I waited at stoplights, driving home, I Googled countries with friendly immigration policies.

€ € €

My car would only hold four or five boxes at a time — two in the trunk, two in the back, one in the passenger's seat. If I didn't fasten the passenger's seatbelt around the box, my dashboard flashed crankily while I drove, and made a sound like I'd left the door open. It took seven trips to move everything into the storage locker.

I looked around my apartment before bed. No men on the futon. No ladies in the shower. No weeping coming from the front closet.

I sent a post out on Facebook expressing that those who wanted to preserve the family artifacts could feel free to contribute to a fund to help pay for storage.

I thought, *I'm turning into one of them.*

On the phone, my mother said, "That's a serious risk. You don't have kids, or a sounding board."

"What?"

"A husband. No one to listen to you. So you get passive-aggressive. Watch out. You'll turn into a martyr."

€ € €

I went on vacation. I kept a website of last-minute discounted vacations bookmarked, and found one for five days, all-inclusive, in the Cayman Islands. Two hundred dollars extra to fly out of Saskatoon. I left two days after clearing my apartment.

I drank fruity rum drinks, and had the midnight buffet. It was impossibly humid. I wore a one-piece bathing suit with a low back, and put my hair up in a chignon whenever I went out to the pool deck. A friendly middle manager put sunscreen on the backs of my thighs.

I felt a lot better.

I went home and the woman was still there.

In the summers, I like to travel, as much as I can with a full-time job. Last year, I went to Greece. I spent ten days touring selected ruins with a small bus-travelling group, and not one manifestation of the weepy dead disturbed me. Greece was full of dead people, but they left me alone. One woman on the bus claimed she was a bit of a psychic, and that she could feel emanations from the ruins. She had cheap plastic dream-catcher earrings. While we were drinking red wine in the post-midnight slump of unmarried women talking about sex, I asked her, *Do you think I could be psychic, too?*

She said, *Come here. Lean back against me.* So I leaned against her, on the banquette in the bar of our hotel, and she took my temples in her hands and pressed on the seams where I'd hardened in the months after birth. She asked me to visualize a journey, and periodically on that journey I came across an object that she asked me to describe. Once, when I hesitated on an answer, she pressed harder and I felt the little cracks where the bones had fused.

Afterwards, she studied me, and said, certainly, it was possible. I could be psychic.

She was utterly lying.

She was a fifty-something lady with plastic earrings, and she felt *bad* for me. "You don't have any children, do you?"

I didn't.

She said, "You should have children. To pass your gift on to." Then she took away my wine and told me to go to bed, and the next day she sat next to a different woman on the bus, and wouldn't pose beside me in group pictures.

I do think she put something in my drinks in the later nights, though. Waiters became friendly. Guys who came to the bars to pick up middle-aged Canadians looking for a quickie became appealing. I made out with one of them, just for fun. We didn't even leave the bar. We shared a padded booth, one with a rounded bench, and I ran my hand along his thigh, and then we both went back to the dancing. The psychic smiled at me.

I sat farther from her. I bought cans of Coke and kept her away from them.

The next time I had sex, it was with a man who ran a genetic-tests-by-mail business, and that was in Canada. We met online, and we had a few dates, and I slept over at his house. His apartment.

It wasn't as nice as mine. It was a real apartment, not owned, in a low-rise building a couple of miles from the university. He wore briefs, and he was younger than me. I felt young compared to him. The next time he called, I made an excuse.

He called again. I made another excuse.

He said, "I thought you wanted a relationship."

"I don't know what I want."

"You said *in your profile* that you wanted a relationship."

"I've changed my profile."

"I'd like to know why you won't take my calls."

The pink-T-shirt woman wandered in from the kitchen. Her T-shirt was over her shoulder, and she was naked to the waist. She'd replaced my coffee with murky instant from some earlier period in history, and she'd mixed in powdered creamer and something that smelled like crème de menthe. I said to him, "I don't want a relationship this badly."

"I beg your pardon."

"Don't call me."

I hung up. I refused to answer the next call. And the next one. He called for several days. I finally phoned my service provider and asked them to block his number. In the meantime, I developed a taste for the coffee she made, and she found a bathrobe to wear while I was in the room.

At night, if I got up to go to the bathroom, she'd be walking around naked in the kitchen. She made revolting casseroles.

I said, "Who are you?"

"Viviene, honey. I was your mom's aunt."

"Viviene died when I was five."

"Life's hard."

"You drank yourself to death."

She looked offended. "I died of cancer."

I went off to the second bedroom — my office, again — and looked it up. "You died of liver failure."

"And cancer."

I said, "What do you *want*?"

"I'm just keeping you company, sweetheart." She paused. "Am I bothering you?"

I was tired. I said, "Yeah, kind of."

She disappeared. She didn't start crying again until I'd gone back to bed.

€ € €

No one donated to the storage-locker fund. I wrote, *Take what you want by May 6th, because that's the last day I'm paying for.*

My mother went by and dug out a box with a few bits of jewellry in it, and a china box, and a porcelain angel. She gave me the box and kept the rest. "Will you take it to the dump?"

"I'm just going to stop paying. They can auction the lot."

"There could be personal information in there."

I didn't think there was much of anything else. I tried to imagine a data thief with the dedication to sort through that mess. He'd find some long-closed bank accounts, the life insurance policies of dead people, and the records of hockey teams my uncles played on in the early 1970s, before their hips and backs started to give out.

The storage company sent me multiple notices. They tried to bill my credit card, but I phoned in and had it cancelled, explaining that I had lost the card and thought someone might be running up bills.

The locker itself I'd put under my great-grandfather's name. At the time, I told them he was moving, and I'd arranged to store a few of his things until he could pick them up. I'm not sure they believed me, but I repeated the story to the bill collectors who phoned to inquire whether I had really, genuinely meant to abandon my responsibilities. What, the man on the phone asked, did that say about me. Say about me as a person?

I said, "I think it says it's not my responsibility, and you need to stop phoning."

He did call back, and then there was a woman, and then they must have decided it wasn't enough money to keep hunting me. It wasn't, I insisted, my locker full of things. If others had abandoned them — maybe they'd died, had they checked whether the owner of the boxes was dead? — I was sorry to hear it. They should check if the owner was dead.

I was fairly confident. He'd died in 1978. If they tracked down that detail, they might come back for me, but I suspected they'd stop with *dead*.

I went for a walk along the traffic-wash by the storage company and saw the poster for their next auction. People stopped their cars and took pictures of the poster, like they'd need the information later.

The day after the auction, I booked another trip. Costa Rica, for next winter, the week of Christmas. I told my parents they could feel free to go somewhere, too. An aunt or two sent me disappointed emails about missing me at dinner. I sent them my most sincere apologies. Tried to picture Christmas without the carefully crafted elf displays and complex appetizers of my nesting family.

Over Christmas, I was inundated with email. Most of it was from cousins who were hoping to go through the locker contents. I didn't answer a single message. I was out of the country. They had no right to expect that I would check my email regularly. I had a sarong and a booked tour to see a waterfall warm enough to shower in, and if I checked my email in the hotel's business centre before we headed out, I doubted any of them could prove it.

It occurred to me that if I scratched the CDs of information, cancelled my Facebook account, maybe spilled coffee on my school reports, that would be the end of it. I made a note to myself on hotel stationery to do all those things, and then blame my mother if anyone called me on it. Or blame a bad boyfriend. Mr. Genetics-By-Mail. He'd been insistent. I'd had to go offline to avoid him.

Definitely. It was completely plausible.

I slept in on Christmas Day, in an air-conditioned room decorated with hideous tropical prints. I had rum drinks and a large slice of ham for lunch. I danced with a divorced man from Calgary by torchlight.

He came back to my room, but didn't sleep over. He left his business card on the night table.

I curled up against a pillow in the night and felt someone stroking my hair, but when I woke up, I found it was Viviene. She'd made herself coffee with the in-room machine. She'd been crying, earlier, but the used tissues were stashed under the bed, so I didn't find them until the next morning.

When I came back at New Year's, there was a typewriter in my second bedroom. The weepy dead had had a party while I was gone. They'd left coffee cups everywhere, and taken pictures of each other. The exposed rolls of film were piled neatly on the table. I ignored them and went to bed, and got up to use the bathroom to a chorus of them crying in the living room, softly, like they hoped I wouldn't notice.

€ € €

My family has emigrated from six different countries. Some of that was in the notes my uncles had kept, that went into the scanned files. We came up from the States most recently, not counting the genealogical branch that settled for a while in Paraguay. They migrated through Mexico, and joined the rest in Canada in my grandparents' generation. Others came directly from Ireland and Germany and the French colonies of the South Pacific.

I tracked that migration through the nights I couldn't sleep. I sleep better at work, now. I come in early, work til noon with carefully logged hours, and then retreat to the ladies' room. If someone comes in to cry — it's winter again, they could just have runny noses, but it sounds like tears — it's brief. I can sleep almost all afternoon before I have to go home.

I haven't been able to retrace anyone's steps. I have to pick a new country. I won't take anything older than myself with me. My mother and my dad can come visit, if they want. If I settle somewhere warm, they might come for whole winters at a time.

I think Greece. I think Costa Rica. I think there has to be a country beyond the disappointed things in my apartment. I should go somewhere new. Find some man whose family is old and complicated. Marry him. If I'm too old to make children with him, well.

Well.

Scatterheart

WHEN NICOLE FIRST CLEANS THE BEDROOM, SHE'S struck by the sheer number of jewellry boxes. She has three of her own, and a little box for earring studs. Mrs. Gamble has every surface of her bedroom covered with boxes. Tacky, plastic ones, mostly, set with iridescent glass gemstones that are oily-reflective at odd angles.

Her best theory is that Mrs. Gamble's kept all her jewellry. All of it she's ever had since she was a little girl. The first box Nicole knocks over provides a certain amount of evidence: it's packed with tangled, broken chains, mostly tarnished. Four-teen-carat gold-plated ones with small pendants, the kind that you can buy in the drugstore around Christmas. Some chains are black enough that underneath they must be silver. Old brooches are mixed in, and clip-on earrings like the ones Nicole remembers seeing in her grandmother's jewellry boxes.

The box that falls is an old one. It's velveteen-lined, and a very small plastic ballerina rotates dissonantly when the case cracks. Nicole realizes she's broken the music box mechanism. She can't even tell what it was supposed to play before she knocked it over.

She shuts the box and doesn't say anything about it.

There are bead-strings that won't fit in the boxes: she finds them on the floor between layers of discarded clothes. They've become part of the house's smell. Even after the clothes are washed and hanging outside, the beads retain a vague body odour.

She says, "Do you want me to clean these?"

Mrs. Gamble, Nicole understands, was sick for a while. She had cancer, though apparently not seriously, but then she fell and broke her leg, up high, and was laid up for months. The home-care aide who came in was only for nursing assistance, and the mess built up. The kitchen grew its own layers, and the laundry failed to wash itself. Milk was absent-mindedly put away with the dishes. Teacups went into the hall closet with the sheets. There's mail all over the living room floor.

This happens. She's seen it on TV. There are programs dedicated to the people whose houses get out of hand, and the heroic British ladies who storm in with a cleaning crew and an arsenal of organic cleansers, and put the house back in order. First, though, they take swabs from the kitchen and bathroom. Grow the germs in a lab until they're exotic, Petri-dish-colour specimens. Explain about the flesh-eating virus lurking behind the toilet because no one scrubbed back there for five or six years. They showcase the *E. coli* in the kitchen.

A little Ebola in the hall rug. Time to have that out, love.

Mrs. Gamble didn't let it get that bad. She might have, but she got better. Pulled herself upright, still partly casted, hobbled off to Friesen's market for real food, and put up a sign on the corkboard looking for cleaning help.

The small poster didn't really make the scale of the problem clear, but Nicole can't blame that on the old lady. The phone number listed wasn't even for Mrs. Gamble. It was for the new lesbian minister who took over St. Andrew's. She visits shut-ins. Maybe she was the one who moved Mrs. Gamble's OxyContin out of the bedroom so that she had to get out of bed and look at the kitchen. The minister's the kind of lady who'd volunteer to organize a home-salvage operation.

Nicole likes the minister, who has a badass, biker-chick aura that's only thinly layered with Christian serenity. She jokes that she was converted on the road to Sturgis, South Dakota.

She was converted by a grandmother with a Turtle Island kind of faith. An old Indian lady who bought her a drink and explained to her that there was work to do, up north, and she'd better get back to it.

"So I went to seminary. Put my name in to come up here."

Nicole moved home after six years in Vancouver, and she likes a minister with a full sleeve of tattoos. Likes that the minister does visits on the reserves that ring the town, and not just at the white people's houses. She does ceremonies, too, if the elders ask her. She's known for not being a cunt about things.

Lesbians drive out from cities four or five hours away to get married in St. Andrew's. It keeps the church open and the minister in biker boots.

After a couple of girls tried cleaning Mrs. Gamble's house and decided maybe they wouldn't, the minister called Nicole and asked her if she wanted the job. Off the books. They'd list it as charity work, with an honorarium, so she wouldn't lose her unemployment.

"There's nothing toxic in there. I sent some swabs to the university labs."

"You watch that show too?"

"Everybody does. Nothing's going to hurt the baby."

It's good enough for her. Nicole is five months, now. She can still bend, as long as she doesn't have to lift anything too heavy, and she can use the money. She's seen worse messes.

In a few months, she thinks, she might live in a worse mess.

Mrs. Gamble goes out to volunteer at the mission store,

downtown, and Nicole comes in while she's out. They don't talk about the mess. Not about the couple of entirely dried and not-really-smelly adult diapers that Nicole finds under the bed. She wouldn't have been mean about it. Mrs. Gamble might be embarrassed, but she was sick. Really sick. Nicole spent a year or so being a serious drunk, a few years back, and she's left bigger stains with less reason. She'll say so if Mrs. Gamble ever looks upset about it.

Accidents happen.

She should tell Mrs. Gamble about the pickles.

Nicole went to a few prenatal classes in the city, and one of the women told her, *If you're worried about your water breaking in public, you should carry around a jar of pickles.*

Nicole thought about this. About the woman talking to her, who had long dark hair and a big smile and didn't look like the type to make obscure dick jokes with multiple fetuses present.

It's so if your water breaks, you can drop the jar. Make sure to really throw it down, so it'll shatter. Then there'll be pickles and pickle brine and mess everywhere, and you can tell people you just dropped some pickles, you didn't wet yourself. You're just really, really embarrassed and you'd like to go now. Like, before the next contraction.

It's too early for this to be an issue, but Nicole has a small jar of sweet bread-and-butter pickles in her backpack. Just for luck.

She makes a thin bath of water and vinegar and soaks the plastic jewelry until it doesn't smell anymore. Rinses it and hangs the bead-strands over the shower rail to dry.

While she's putting things away in the bedroom, she finds the other boxes.

There are a few pretty stone-and-metal boxes, biggish, from the Mennonite import store, that don't weigh much. She thought they might hold the beads after they dry.

One box is filled with ashes. One with paper. One has dried meat in it.

Nicole looks at the dried meat. It isn't jerky. Her grandmother used to store moose jerky in old boxes, in between pieces of waxed paper, but that was in strips. This is a single, hard lump. It smells like metal.

She closes the box. Puts it back where she found it.

Then she finds a handful of dust in the corner of the back bedroom, where she hasn't cleaned yet, and rubs it onto each box, so they look untouched.

Goes home without locking the door and washes her hands a few times.

Calls the minister.

The minister's cell goes straight to voicemail. Nicole grabs some hand sanitizer and a bottle of diet Coke, goes over to sit in the church.

Nicole never did get saved, exactly. She doesn't believe in it. It's more that when she pulled herself together, in Vancouver, she spent some time on the phone with one of her aunts, who said prayers for her at the Ste-Anne shrine. Made her a prayer bundle out of rosary beads and some of her favourite CDs she'd left behind. Burned a candle and some sage.

She always liked that.

She didn't, when she got back, like the priest at the shrine. He wasn't resident; he'd come up from somewhere in the far south, and he wasn't impressed with any of it. He cleaned house. Complained about pagans and heresy.

The lesbian minister crawled into the trash bins and rescued everybody's prayer bundles. She set them up on a side table in St. Andrew's, let people come and take them away if they wanted. Nicole came to pick up her aunt's stuff, and she liked the minister, who gave her a can of diet Coke and talked with her for two hours about the college-circuit punk scene, and then offered to help Nicole dye her hair back to some colour a little more human.

Not that she wasn't pretty, blonde. But it didn't look like her.

Nicole doesn't know how the minister knew what she really looked like, but she let her. Leaned over the sink in the rectory and let a strange, butch lesbian punk dye her hair dark, dark red.

She likes to think her baby might have reddish hair. Reddish black. It'll be pretty.

Nicole thinks about this and not about meat until Mrs. Gamble says, from behind her, "You found my heart."

Nicole pees, just a little. Her maternity panties absorb it, and she clamps down. Stands up with as much dignity as she can.

The minister's off in the corner, setting the remaining prayer assemblages to rights. They live here now. She says most of the old people just ignore them. Or they say something racist enough that she earns the right to explain to them exactly how specific Jesus was about loving one's neighbour, and also about post-colonial injustice, and leaves them to think about that. Pray on it.

Mrs. Gamble says, "It's my heart."

"No."

"It's my heart. You know my daughter died?"

"No."

"My daughter died of scarlet fever. In 1968."

"Nobody dies of scarlet fever," says Nicole. Except, her uncle Mike died of it, she thinks. But that was before she was born.

"Anyone can die of scarlet fever. It's strep throat gone terribly, terribly wrong."

"They had antibiotics then." She's almost sure.

Mrs. Gamble looks at her flatly. "I know. Nonetheless, she died. She was seven." She sways on her crutch. Mrs. Gamble isn't fully mobile, but she's rejected an electric scooter as a symptom of the mess in her home. Unless she has the pills concealed on her body, she's given up OxyContin, too. "She was my heart."

Nicole blinks. "You have your daughter's heart in a box?"

"I asked for it. People understand, if you ask the right way."

Nicole thinks about this. She says, "The box isn't that old."

"I replace it every few years. You were raised Catholic. Latin: *Vide cor meum*."

"I don't think that's Latin."

From the corner, the minister says, "Technically, she's right, Hannah. It's Italian. Dante, not the Bible. But I take your meaning." To Nicole, she says, "It means, *Behold my heart*. From *La Vita Nuova*, The New Life."

Mrs. Gamble says, mildly, "I prefer *The Life to Come* as a translation."

"Mine is more accurate."

"I don't like this," says Nicole.

"Many people keep ashes in an urn."

"She has those, too."

"Those are my husband."

Nicole says, "I think you should clean your own house, if you're going to keep pieces of your family in it." She leaves.

She stays home the next day. She has a headache, and there's nothing she can do, really, except lay a cloth over her eyes and lie in the dark. She read about what pills, even over-the-counter pills, can do to babies, and decided she wouldn't take anything during her pregnancy. Not even ibuprofen. As long as she keeps the blinds closed and the lights off, she can even stagger to the bathroom, and get herself crackers and Powerade when she's desperate.

She drinks the clear Powerade flavour. Strawberry-kiwi, but it tastes like no colour at all, and except for the sugar-salt smell, it could be water. When Nicole had morning sickness, she tried drinking the fruit punch kind, but the red in her vomit scared her. She'd thrown up so long she wasn't sure she wasn't bleeding, and they kept her overnight in the hospital, just to be sure. Afterwards, she cut food colouring out of her diet.

It's safer this way. Mostly, she cooks her own food, from scratch. If she wants red foods, she cooks tomatoes. Thinks about how her grandmother called them *love apples*.

When she's sick like this, she can't cook. She eats crackers and takes vitamins and waits to feel better. If she disappears, the minister will come looking to make sure she isn't dead.

The minister doesn't come, though. Mrs. Gamble comes, with a nylon bag and a sealer-jar of chicken soup.

"I haven't cleaned your kitchen yet," Nicole says. Not thoroughly, with bleach. The room is septic. Old bananas and forgotten dairy products have fused on the counter. She wouldn't make tea for the dead in there.

"I made it at the rectory. She likes my cooking, Pastor Marilyn."

The soup is real, made with animal carcass and half-dried vegetables, and it tastes like salt and maybe a little like blood. Nicole drinks four or five spoonfuls before she thinks about the meat in the jewelry box.

"Only chicken, sweetheart."

Nicole swirls her spoon. It turns up translucent onion and pale meat shreds. She sips again. It still tastes like blood, but that might only be her headache. She pushes the bowl away and gets up, walks away from Mrs. Gamble without saying anything. She needs to lie down. Curl up in her bedroom and try to stay very, very still.

She has almost no short-term memory when her head

hurts like this. She's startled when Mrs. Gamble comes in, because she forgot there was anyone else in the house.

"Could you bear a light in the hallway?"

"I don't know."

"Let's try."

Nicole turns her face away from it. The light's not strong enough to penetrate her eyelids. She cracks one open. The light's like a thin trickle added to bathwater; she can't tell yet whether it's warm or cold.

Mrs. Gamble comes to sit in front of her. She has the orange nylon bag with her, held in her lap.

"It didn't occur to me that you'd open the boxes."

"I'm sorry."

"Mmmm. Well. Behold my heart, no?"

Only, when Nicole cracks her eye open again, she really is. Beholding the heart. Mrs Gamble has the box open on her lap and the dried heart lies in her cupped hands.

"Oh God."

"She died before you were born. I wasn't ready for it."

"Please put it away."

She can hear the metal of the lid slide into place. She thinks she might smell smoke.

"This is my husband. A man will leave his father and his mother, and be united to his wife, and the two will become one flesh."

Nicole doesn't open her eyes. She's sure she smells smoke. Thick air. Ashes.

Mrs. Gamble is quiet for a while. Then she says, "This is the baby I lost."

"Please go away."

"She wasn't ever alive, really. I suppose she was four months or so. Now they count the weeks."

Nicole is twenty-five weeks pregnant. She can count the days. One hundred and two to go.

"I thought of burying her in the back garden. I'm not sure, really, that she was a girl. But she came after my other daughter, so I thought, maybe."

"Please. Please. Go away."

"I would like you to come back. You were good for my home."

"I don't think you're good for me."

"If you never saw them again," Mrs. Gamble says, "then could you bear it?"

So Nicole does go back, when her headache eases. Not to lift anything else, but with nontoxic cleansers she can at least do the dishes properly, and fold the clean sheets. All the jewellry boxes are gone. The bedroom is spotlessly clean, and very bare. She's made an effort, Mrs. Gamble has. She's found a boxful of mystery novels from the book exchange to sit on her dresser, to look like clutter.

Nicole wipes the counters down with vinegar. She washes the dishes by hand in very hot water, wearing gloves and soaking away the growths on the edges of plates.

The minister pays Nicole the honorarium. Mrs. Gamble gives her carnations and a small beaded bracelet that seems to have come from the Mennonite import store and not her own stock. A thank-you present when Nicole officially finishes cleaning the house and formally goes on maternity leave.

And then she waits. Two weeks. Ten days. Eight. Five.

She thinks about Vancouver. How it smells nothing like Swanson.

She's in Friesen's market, buying apple juice and crackers, when she feels the first contraction. Just a slight pain. She digs in her pocket for her phone, makes a note of the time. Waits for the next one. It doesn't come, immediately, so she puts the phone away and keeps shopping. Puts back anything perishable, but she's going to need food. If she leaves a few dollars with Pastor Marilyn, she might stock Nicole's fridge with whole milk for the day after tomorrow. Or the day after that.

Her belly tightens.

And then she's wet, very suddenly, and not in the pickle aisle. She has to dig in her bag, instead, for the jar. She takes hold and hurls it at the ground, quick before anyone sees her.

Nothing to see here. Just pickles.

Except, the smell isn't sweet or briny. More like pure vinegar.

Her oceanic smell is underneath that, but when she looks down, Nicole doesn't see pickles. The jar that's smashed on the floor was a little bigger, and much older. A sealer jar.

Mrs. Gamble was right. She can't really tell whether it was a girl. But she's surrounded by broken glass. Her belly contracts again.

She stares at the dead thing, pickled and ancient, on the market floor. Tries to decide how she's going to get out the door with this smell all over her clothes.

You Are Not
Needed Now

WHEN KRISTA FIRST STARTED COMING TO THE track, she wore heels and a jean skirt. No nylons, obviously. But in heels she could only go as far as the clubhouse. She could sit in the bar, drinking dollar-fifty diet Cokes and cuddling up to happy-looking older guys, the ones who were winning. She could walk across a parking lot, but she couldn't jump a fence. Couldn't go back into the barns.

The guys in the bar were steady customers, mostly, but the older ones made her skin crawl, and they offered her crumpled twenties pulled out of their front pockets. Or they asked her to reach in and take them.

Working at the track wasn't as bad as she thought it would be, really. She hadn't gone, before. She'd been working at a trucking company, mostly on dispatch, and that was a good job. She could chat with the drivers, sometimes, once they installed the hands-free system. They'd tell her jokes, and she'd cross-reference their GPS location with the next Tim Hortons, or Starbucks, if that was what they liked. Gave a few of them a hard time about half-soy lattes ruining their trucker-physiques. There was an office cat.

She knows that good jobs don't always last, but it was shit when they laid her off. Not enough business to maintain non-family staff members. They offered to give her a decent reference, if she needed one.

The cashier jobs she was looking at paid minimum wage. She worked two of them, and then she got the flu and had to stay home for almost a week.

So it goes, her boss said. Like it meant something. But they'd replaced her.

And then her buddy Mike's ex-girlfriend offered to take Krista with her to the track a few times. Just to feel it out, see if it was something she could do, until she thought of something better.

It's not, Jamie explained, anything like working downtown. It's not street-walking. The guys who go to the track are always there, and they have extra money sometimes, and most of them are divorced, or else they were always single. They're not good at finding girlfriends. They like to dance. They'll take you out for a cheap steak at one of the bars on Portage, and waltz you around the floor if there's a country band playing, and if you sleep with them, they'll give you a handful of bills that pay your bills, and it's a good night out. They're old-fashioned cowboys.

They're not, Krista finds out, really very clean, most of the time. Like they forgot about daily showers about ten years ago. Up close they smell like beer. But Jamie's not wrong about the dancing.

Krista doesn't know how to waltz. It should be a deal-breaker, but she finds that some of the guys love teaching her to dance. Like it's one of only maybe three things they do really well. Settle her into·dance-frame, and they whisper in her ear, *slow quick-quick, slow quick-quick.* Push her gently around the tiny dance floor. Once she learns how, Krista still pretends she can't, with new customers. Lets them teach her, and only "remembers" how to dance with regulars.

She doesn't learn to shuffle or polka, but the foxtrot's easier than she expects.

Jamie calls her "dance-hall girl." Buys her a stained crinoline at Value Village and hangs it on Krista's closet door.

She wears it for this messy old cowboy who calls her up sometimes. Layers it under the square-dancing outfit he brings her piece by piece. Dances with him in his trailer, out on Highway 6, and rides his lap on his fuzzy floral couch. She drives herself, picks up and goes home after, but the one time she falls asleep with her head in his lap, he makes her coffee and scrambled eggs for breakfast.

He pays her twenty bucks less than the others, though, so if something better comes along, she won't see him for weeks.

Weekends, party nights, those are good. But she's at the track almost every day. The bar manager asks her for a blowjob, and after she gives it to him he doesn't give her steady trouble. And he introduces her to Terry, who keeps three or four horses on the track at a time, and lives in the camper on his truck during the racing season.

Terry's older than she is, but abstractly, like she couldn't guess his real age. He never has any money, and she isn't going to fuck him for free. But he takes her down the back stairs with him, uses his swipe card to open the back door and takes her into the stables.

Because of Terry, Krista comes to work now in high-heeled boots and cut-offs. They still show her legs, and she can wiggle out of the shorts easily enough, but she can't ride with a skirt on.

⇐ ⇐ ⇐

Jamie says, "If I move downtown, can you take care of yourself?"

"How is downtown better than this?"

"Uptown, then. I didn't mean literally downtown. Just, a friend of mine's doing outcalls for business guys in the downtown hotels, and she wants a second for when they ask for two girls."

Krista tries to picture this. Not the two girls, because she's run across enough porn videos to give her a fairly good idea of how that would work, but Jamie playing the call girl. Thigh-high stockings and lacy underwear under a trench coat. Sitting on a stool in downtown hotel bars where you aren't even allowed to smoke. It sounds lonely.

This last weekend, Krista decided she wanted a tattoo. Her first one, her date said. He looked like he might have been in a punk band, but the first time punk came around. Long and skinny and hard skin, but he had two sleeves of not-biker tattoos, and she hadn't seen a guy that age with multiple piercings before. Stretched ear lobes.

She told him she wanted a tattoo.

"How many do you have?"

"None."

He grinned. "Virgin."

"Sure." Really, why not?

"Can I watch?"

She snorted. "If you want."

Only, instead of asking if he could fuck her first, he dragged her into a booth with a plate of fries, and said, "What's the design?"

She hadn't thought about it, really. "A dolphin?"

"Please God, no."

"A horse." She used to draw horses in the margins of her notebooks. Learned to shape the pasterns and the right balance to draw one rearing.

He studied her. Said, "On the whole, animals are a bad idea. Think harder." Like a teacher looking over her shoulder.

"Horses."

"Better." And he started drawing, on her arm with a ballpoint pen. Not one big horse, but a herd of tiny ones, running strung out from her wrist to her elbow. "That could work."

"I don't want it on my arm."

"Sweetheart," he said, cheesy like television, "you can get it anywhere you like."

He wasn't joking about that. Not just about her skin, but about where she could get it. He had opinions about tattoos like the other guys had opinions about beer and horses, and waltz tempos. Told her she shouldn't ever get a tattoo anywhere that would do it the same night. Only, he could set her up, with his buddy.

He took her downtown, over the bridges and the rivers to this strip mall place next to a French-language liquor store. Sat with her in the too-bright lights until the sleepy counter girl went to close up, then dragged his buddy out of the back. Big biker dude with a moustache. Said, "Do her."

He paid for it, so he got to watch. Watch her peel off her blouse and shorts and lie down in her underwear on the vinyl couch. He got to draw the pattern on her, freehand, with a blue marker. Horses running from her ribcage down to her right hip. Kissed her when he was finished. Pulled her up into his lap and rocked her there, smudging the ink guide-lines with his sweaty hand, and when he took his tongue out of her mouth, he asked if she wanted something.

"Like food?"

"Like painkillers." He had a crushed sandwich bag with pills in it. Little yellow round ones and long, fat white tablets. "Lets you think about something other than the needles."

She'd had a rye and Coke with him earlier, and she wasn't really drunk, just lightly buzzed. She'd checked "no" on the form that asked whether she was intoxicated before she signed the consent.

She let him kiss her again with a yellow circle on his tongue and pass it into her mouth.

She remembers the needles being very sharp for about ten minutes. After that, she didn't care so much. Lost track of how she felt about it, except good and a little sleepy, and when the biker dude said, "You're done, sweetheart," she was surprised.

Crawled into punk-boy's lap in the cab of his half-ton in the parking lot and started grinding. He laughed at her. Pushed her off of him and then pulled her head down. Hummed happily while she blew him. He had grey hair around his dick, but he was clean, cleaner than the last three guys she'd blown. He only left twenty bucks in her pocket when he dropped her near the Perimeter Highway, but she was staggering and couldn't really figure out what to say about that. He gave her two more of the yellow pills, and a white one, and told her she was gorgeous. That he'd do her better next time.

Jamie looks at the pills when Krista shows her. Says she'll get her friend to look them up. Later, she buzzes Krista's phone.

two oxy one vicodin nice

Krista shoves them down to the bottom of her bag. In case of emergency. There with her pack of "the pill," and the coloured condoms and the normal ones, and the latex gloves she picked up at Shoppers.

Days it rains, there are actually more people in the bar. There are no local races, but the simulcasts run all afternoon, and old ladies wander in to play the VLTs. The women watch her far more closely than the men do, except when they're actually looking for a date. It means Krista has to sit down, pull her knees up under her chin, and watch the races. As soon as she walks the room, one lady or another gets up, actually abandoning the machine she's staked out for hours, and goes to complain. About the *lady of the night*. And then Krista has to actually leave, go down and lurk in the barns, or just go home and sleep. Wait to see if any of the regulars phone.

If she stays quiet, sometimes they come looking for her. The guys who wouldn't ever call her for a date, because it has to be an accident every time they hook up. They're older, mostly. If she thinks about it actively, they remind her of her dad, so she doesn't think about actively. She makes rules, even. About *who's your daddy?* and *sugar-daddy* and *my little girl*. You say that, she stops. It's the end of the blowjob. The end of the fuck.

As often as she can manage it, it's the end. If she can't end it, she writes everything about the guy she can remember into her phone (*big gut/beer hat, moustache creeper, smells like dentist's office*), and if he comes looking for her after that, she has bear spray in her purse to stand him off.

She isn't quite prepared for him to be waiting by her car, at night. Long July evening, and it's not quite dark, but the track's officially closed, and she's walking by herself. Looking at this dirty, pushy asshole sitting against her driver's side door. Grinning at her like he just fucked the queen.

He says, "I missed you."

"Fuck off."

"Come on. I missed you. Come to daddy."

So then, *then* she has to spray him. Backs up as far as she can, for space, finds the can by feel. Pulls the safety ring off. Hits him in the face with capsicum concentrate, hard enough and close enough that the blow-back knocks her down. Like her whole face is on fire. Like murderous chili poured down over her. Asshole's on the ground, half-screaming, but she's shattered. She can't drive.

She runs. Cuts back around the barrier fence and under the chain, both hands over her face, and runs for the watering hydrant. Buries her face in the bone-cold chlorinated rush. Jesus. Jesus fuck it hurts. She throws up, head still under the water, and the chunks of bar food flow away around her bare knees.

Behind her, Terry says, "Do you still have the can?"

She nods. It's in her hand. She never closed her purse; there's water all in it now, and probably vomit. She can't let go.

Terry says, "Give it to me."

Shakes her head.

"No, give it to me. I'm going to throw it away in the ma-nure bins, because nobody's going to dig through there, okay?" He's down on his heels, looking at her. "Okay?" She won't give it to him, but he pries her fingers off the little spray bottle. He has work gloves on, and a bandana over most of his face. Like she's been sprayed by a skunk. Like she's soaked in chlorine gas. "You have to throw it away. They called an ambulance for him. They're going to look for you. So you throw it away, and then maybe you never saw that guy, if any-body asks. You stopped by to see me. We had a beer. Talked about horses. And you got some fly spray in your eyes, and we washed you off."

Krista throws up again.

Terry walks away with the can. Comes back. "You're supposed to spray the bears from twelve feet away, minimum. That shit'll turn a grizzly if she's only half pissed off."

He hauls her up, drags her back toward the barns. If he wanted to fuck her, there wouldn't be any way she could stop him. Her bear spray's gone. She can't open her eyes. Her face feels like it's covered in angry bees.

It's all very sexy. But she has no idea, really, what Terry's kinks are. There's porn for everything, so there must be perverts for everything.

If he has kinks, they're about water. He takes away her purse, pulls off her boots, and pushes her into what she finds out later is a wash stall. Hoses her down like an animal. Comes in close with a bottle and starts rubbing her.

Through her swollen face, she says, "Smells like fries."

"Good nose. Vegetable oil. Alcohol's next."

"Kinky fucker."

"I used to cowboy in the BC Interior. I've seen a face-full of bear spray before."

She throws up three more times. She smells like fries for two days.

€ € €

Krista's too fat to be a jockey, but Terry lets her ride during training. Says she calms the horses down. They need exercise, and when the skinny fuckers he hires ride them in races, the horses are so startled by the weight shift they run harder.

He doesn't call her fat. She knows she is because he keeps a weight requirements chart taped to the camper door's inside, and the numbers for rider and saddle together are less than she's weighed since she was about twelve. Even when she was on a diet kick, she was never that skinny.

"You're better off strong," is what he tells her. She can fight a scared horse back down from a dead run. If he had the money, he'd hire her to pony-ride the race horses in, because she's strong enough to catch one and pull it down if the jockey can't get her stopped.

Terry does that part himself. On race days, he goes out on this Appaloosa gelding he bought at an auction, leading the hysterical thoroughbreds. Just sort of cowboy-shaped. The rest of the track's full English, like they'd export the whole thing back to Europe if they could. So he stands out.

The other owners, some of them, have money. They're lawyers who like horses enough to keep them as a hobby, but they don't ride, or not on the track. One of them tells her he plays polo, north of the city, on alternate weekends. That he likes the speed.

"This is mostly for clients," he says, nodding at the track. The horses have been running all afternoon, and the lawyer bought Krista a drink and paid for a handjob, then wanted to show her his stable. "So I can take them out."

By stable, he means the horses he keeps at the track. He hired a couple of guys to take care of them, and train them. His polo ponies board by the polo grounds.

"You don't have a farm?" Krista asks him.

"I had one for a bit. The commute was too much trouble." He pats her hand. "Are you around here much?"

Krista looks at him for a minute. "How about I give you my friend's number?"

"I want yours. I'd like to take you to see a polo game."

She says, "I'm around."

But later she gives him Jamie's cell number, and he really does like her. He calls her *classy*. And he pays her about two hundred dollars at a time, so Jamie kicks a few bucks back over to Krista now and then, and they don't say anything about him liking tanned white girls with frosted hair a bit better than he liked Krista.

"And you can be, you know, in *Pretty Woman*."

But Jamie says the polo grounds are just this field on the edge of the provincial park where a bunch of guys get together and play sometimes. They've got one horse each, or maybe two. "I looked it up," says Jamie, "and for real you're supposed to have, like, six horses. If you're in the royal family, or if you're Tommy Lee Jones, and you play for serious."

It comes out, eventually, that the lawyer killed his wife. He hired two bikers to do it, and they turned him in when they were picked up for dealing. Jamie and this redhead get busted at his riverview condo when the police come to arrest him, and they all have their pictures on the cover of the *Sun*, and for a couple of weeks it's really embarrassing.

Jamie says to Krista, when she calls, "How about you don't do me any more favours."

"He didn't look like he killed his wife."

"I'm not finished being mad at you, okay? So don't call me for a while."

It means, though, that Krista hasn't really got anyone to call. It snows in the first week of October, and she has to decide whether it's worth coming in to the track, and if it is, what she should wear. Not shorts. So she goes back to wearing a skirt, and her boots, and her parka with the hood pulled up. The bar manager quits so he can move up to Fort McMurray, and one of her cowboy-clients has a heart attack and has to move in with his daughter, and the best dance bar on Portage changes formats so that now it plays mostly R&B music that nobody from the track can dance to.

But really, when was winter ever *not* shit? If she was rich, Krista would move somewhere hot, like Mexico, along the coast, and go swimming in the ocean.

When she tells Terry this, he says, "Go somewhere with horses. Have you seen those pictures of people riding on the beach?"

"You've done that?"

"No. I went to Monterrey a couple times, but just with friends. But it kinda always seemed like a good idea. I saw this ad once for a resort in Hawaii where you can do it. Costs thirty-eight hundred bucks for a week. Per person."

She finds that ad in a magazine. Somebody from upstairs in her apartment building moved out, and their mail isn't getting forwarded. The new person just throws the lost mail in a pile on the floor by the mailboxes. Sometimes Krista goes through it, just for magazines and Sephora coupons and sometimes Shoppers catalogues that suggest all the things she could do with expensive makeup. They're fun to read, when she's soaking in her tiny green bathtub with *Dora the Explorer* bubble bath suds around her knees. Nobody ever got arrested just for magazines.

There are bank statements and stuff, but she leaves those. Krista hasn't got much idea how you steal someone else's identity. And if she was going to steal one, she'd steal the identity of someone who lived in a nicer building. Or a house. She should go out to one of the country post offices and steal the identity of someone with a farm. Instead, she cuts the Hawaii ad out and glues it to some cardboard. Gives it to Terry.

"Krista, do you wanna be my girlfriend?"

"That's not why I gave it to you."

"No, but do you?"

She says, "Don't do me any favours, asshole."

And she still does okay. Sometimes she even prints up resumes at the job-finding centre downtown and sends them out, but the best offer she got was for cashiering at a dollar store on the other side of town, and the bus fare each way would eat half of what she'd earn.

She meets this divorced hockey-dad who pays her fifty

bucks to dress in his ex-wife's clothes and go to the rink with him. He buys them fries and coffee. She sits beside him on carpet samples laid over the plywood bleachers and they watch peewee hockey games. His kids moved with his wife to Kitchener-Waterloo. He talks to them on Skype almost every day, but he says he misses the games. And he doesn't want anyone to think he's a pervert. If she's willing to stay overnight sometimes, and let him dry-hump her ass, he makes it two fifties, bright red and hologrammed.

€ € €

It doesn't happen at the track, but Terry gets in a wreck. He's on the highway, on his way back to Boissevain, and the oncoming driver hits a deer and skids across the road, broadsiding him.

The Mountie who comes to pick Krista up says, "It's like physics, you know? That camper's all top-heavy, and then he gets hit from the side, and there's the snow . . ."

Krista says, "I'm fucking *grieving* here."

"Oh, he's not dead. Just kinda bent up. He had your name listed in his wallet, next to his health card, so when they decided to transfer him back to Winnipeg, they had me call you."

He says it like he's waiting for her to say *thank you*, since he's giving her a ride downtown. She doesn't even have to take the bus. She doesn't say it. Just sits. After a while, the Mountie says, "Anyway, I'm supposed to pick up a prisoner at Health Sciences and take him back to Stony Mountain, so you're on my way. It's no problem."

His accent is strange, and eventually, while they're stuck in traffic by Polo Park, he tells her how he's from New Brunswick, and this is only his third month on the prairies. That his girlfriend broke up with him when he was transferred and he doesn't quite know how to meet people now.

Krista says, "You should try the Internet. It works for all kinds of people."

"I can't have your phone number?"

He has her phone number. He called her, from Headingley, to tell her what was going on. But she knows what he means. And he's clean, but he's not any fun, probably. He has a Catholic medal on, and he looks like a guy who'd talk a lot about Jesus, and possibly be really upset about his girlfriend working at the racetrack.

She says, "Let's see if my boyfriend dies. If he does, I'll let you know."

€ € €

On his farm, Terry has a bunch of horses who more or less take care of themselves in the summer, and a cat. In the snow, all the animals hunch together by the old barn. They look up whenever Krista comes outside. Waiting for her to feed them. It's part of the contract. Basic farm chores, plus non-medical home care duties.

Terry used to keep the race horses separate from the saddle horses and the couple of scruffy ponies he says he can't sell. But he didn't set things up before the wreck, and he says he can't expect Krista to cater to the whims of livestock. Not after the goat arrived. "The neighbours moved to BC, and they couldn't find a buyer."

This is also the explanation for the six chickens roosting in the haystack. Terry doesn't justify the family of domestic rabbits, except that "they're good cat food."

On Tuesdays and Thursdays, she helps Terry across the

yard to the new-old truck and drives him into Brandon for physiotherapy. The truck is shit, but it's what his insurance on the old truck bought. He tried to do that by himself, in Winnipeg. On crutches, and high on pain meds. After he had to give up the first truck because it was actually on a lease to the guy who sold it, he phoned Krista.

"I have thirty bucks. If I give it to you, will you come with me?"

He meant, she found out, to pick out a truck. She was mobile, and she was sober. She didn't know anything about trucks, but she phoned up a client who had a yard full of them and he gave Terry a deal and Krista a bag of fancy jelly beans.

A month later, in the middle of a blizzard, Terry asked her to come take care of him.

The deal, she understands, is that she's officially Home Support. His case worker came out to assess him and said he qualified for care, but they didn't have anyone in the area. So instead the province pays Krista for sixteen hours a week to make sure the house doesn't burn down, and that Terry gets a bath once in a while.

This is nowhere. She can almost see over the American border from Terry's yard, and farther if she takes out one of the horses. The physio round trip is three hours. Terry's working on that, on the phone, to see if he can get her paid for the driving hours.

She has her own room.

Terry lives in a trailer on this old, old farm that he says used to belong to his grandpa. The house is more or less falling down, so when Terry came back from working in Alberta, when he bought his first racehorse, he got the mobile home too, and moved it onto the place. It isn't as insulated as it should be, but he rigged a wood stove in the living room. Half the time, Krista sleeps out there on the couch, close to the heat source. If the fire dies down in the night, she can build it up again.

She goes out to feed the horses in the dark, sometimes, if she wakes up too early.

The night she slips on the ice while carrying firewood in, Terry gives her half a Vicodin and sits with her on the couch, rubbing her feet. He can do that. He just can't, like, walk. Not by himself, though his physiotherapist says by spring, he'll for sure be mobile enough to shower all by himself.

In the meantime, he has a bath chair. Krista helps him into the bathroom, and leaves him to get his own boxers off. Except, he falls off. Yells for her and then just howls until she comes back. She throws a towel on him, then wrestles him up.

Terry says, "What would it take for you to just, like, stay here and help me?"

Krista thinks about it, sometimes. She thinks it was a real question.

The cat crawls up between them on the couch. "Who feeds him when you're away?" she asks.

"He eats the delicious rabbits. There'd be a million of them, otherwise. And he hunts. One summer I mostly stayed out here, and I didn't see him more than three times."

Krista doesn't quite believe him, but maybe the cat was more mobile then, too. It's this tatty old orange tom who insinuated himself into the trailer as soon as he worked out that Terry wasn't quick enough to boot him out anymore. He follows Krista around the yard when she's doing chores. Gets up on the fence and touches noses with the horses. Eight horses. One goat. Rabbits that he only catches and chews on a little, then lets go. When she goes in, he's right on her heels.

In the morning, Krista says, "A horse."

Terry nods. "Which one?"

"I don't care. Not one of the ponies, though; one I can ride."

He gives her his track Appaloosa. The big gelding's legal name, it turns out, is Huckabee's Dead Flowers. Terry gives her the pedigree in a plastic sleeve, and carefully signs the blank on the back that makes the horse legally hers. He says, "I guess I'll need you to come work for me next summer."

"You can't afford me."

"I'll think of something."

She helps him into the shower, settles him on the bath chair, and then kneels in front of him to strip his shorts off. Up close, his cock's not really distinct from his balls. His pubic hair's pale brown, and it smells a bit.

Terry says, "I have trouble reaching all over sometimes. I'm sorry about the smell."

She stays in the shower with him, in her bra and panties, and lets the water get very hot. Scrubs him all over with the shower puff and Ivory Liquid Aloe soap, then washes his hair. There are marks along his ribs that look older than the car accident. Up close, his legs are ugly, and she can see the bone pins showing. "Whenever I take a bath, it reminds me of every horse I ever knew."

Krista says, "Yeah."

She's wet, but he's shivering cold. He was always a skinny guy, but now he looks like he might starve to death if she forgets to make him lunch. She can't ever get him warm enough. Her best plan is just to wrap him in all the dry towels she can find, and maybe the fleece blanket from his bed, and lay him out on the couch until his shivering stops.

The wood stove helps, too, when he's close enough to it. Krista walks past him to heat up some soup. Her jeans are still on the bathroom floor. She leaves them there. The fire's steady, and in the kitchen she's warm enough without them.

Terry falls asleep before the soup is ready. Krista has hers at the dinette table and leaves his in the pot until he wakes up. When she goes to settle at the other end of the couch, he shifts restlessly. Rolls onto his side painfully, and looks at her through half-closed, drug-glazed eyes. Krista thinks about the Oxy pill that's crushed into dust at the bottom of her purse. Instead, she lies down beside him under the fleece. The towels around Terry are almost dry.

They sleep that way all afternoon.

When You Tilt Your Head Just So The World Will Crack

WHEN THEY PULLED IN AT SNAKE RIVER AND THE bus driver said they'd be there for fifteen minutes, so go smoke if you want but don't wander too far, David ran across the road to the laundromat and liquor store that was somehow still open. He took the cash he had, and the bills and bigger coins Robin scrounged out of her purse. They'd agreed they wouldn't use plastic, because that would only get them into trouble. He said, "I'll get whatever we can afford, that doesn't smell too much."

He brought back some fruity coolers that could pass for high-class sodas, and a flask of vodka that they decanted into Sprite bottles behind the gas station, out of the driver's sight. Robin used her Visa in the gas station to buy strawberry licorice and pretzels. She got some cheap root beers, too, in plastic bottles.

David said, "Those won't mix."

"I know. But I always used to get root beer for sleepovers, and I wanted some."

They had taken over the back seat of the bus. David was sleeping there when Robin got on, and she'd watched him through the later afternoon, listening to music on her phone, before the battery died. Now their pillows and blankets covered the bench so no one could claim they'd thought the space wasn't taken.

And it was like a sleepover. Bus trips were something you did in pyjama pants, if you could, and you needed your own pillow. Anyone going as far as David was — from Fort St. John to Hamilton — needed a blanket, too. He'd never get comfortable under his coat. He thought the trip would be a bit less than three days total.

When Robin checked his tickets, though, he was wrong about that. It was three days, four hours, twenty-five minutes. Five transfers. He was already on his second leg. He'd change again in Edmonton, but then not again until Winnipeg. Almost a whole day on the bus.

Robin said, "I'm going to be with you until Winnipeg," like it was a big present, a surprise. She thought she sounded like she had in high school, when she'd found out she was going to be in the same homeroom as a friend. *We'll be together, whatever else happens.*

When one of the oil field guys staggered back through the bus to use the can, he looked into Robin and David's corner and said, "You guys look cozy."

"It's okay."

"Wish I wasn't travelling alone. How long have you two been together?"

David said, "Since about Rocky Mountain View."

Robin could see for a minute the guy thought it was a joke. Then he snorted, like he got it. "You lucky bastard," he said to David. "I wish I'd claimed the back seat."

"You snooze you lose . . . the girl."

Robin thought the guy maybe left the door to the tiny toilet stall open on purpose. Like he hoped she might look at his dick and reconsider. She turned her face away and leaned on David's chest. Poked him to start up the movie on his phone again. He had a whole bunch of booster batteries. He figured he'd have power most of the way home, even if he couldn't find a place to charge.

Robin had been single something like thirteen months. She'd gone up to Cut Hand, on the BC border, with Terry, who had a job driving a truck for a natural gas company. There were jobs there for her, too, but they didn't pay anything like his job did. He got in good with the guys who worked in drilling, and started calling himself a *fracker* way before he moved out to the camp to do fracking for real.

It meant he was gone for two weeks at a time. He stayed in his friend Jorden's trailer, because you could save your subsistence money that way. They cooked mostly hot dogs and ate canned peaches so they wouldn't get scurvy. Terry played video games on Jorden's system, networked with the other guys in the camp. They had these huge tournaments that went on all night.

Those long nights, probably, were where a lot of Terry's money went. You could get anything you wanted in the camps, if you had money. Most of the time, Terry managed his half of the rent on their place in town, but he never had anything left over.

"What was he into?" David asked her.

Cocaine, she told him. Just like Terry was some kind of

eighties rock star. He had a mirror he snorted it off. He said it made him sharper in the tournaments.

He didn't use all the time. When he came home he was mostly straight. He slept a lot. Played other game tournaments, online, to up his skill set for camp matches. They had sex a couple of times, maybe, in the two weeks he was home, and then he went off again, and Robin was alone with Facebook and cable TV.

She went out some. Because of the money around town, decent bands came to the bars. She made a few friends, partying. Most of the girls her age were married, though, and had a couple of kids. People had crazy numbers of kids up there — three and four and even five, like it was the fifties or something. Their husbands worked out in the camps, too, but they stayed in their own part of the trailer city. They had prayer meetings.

David said, "Where I was, you were either into junk or Jesus."

Robin liked how still David was. He was awake, and paying attention to their conversation, but he wasn't jittery. His skin didn't twitch if she touched him for too long. He didn't have track marks or the messed-up teeth she associated with guys who worked in gas fields. "Which one did it for you?"

"I faked Jesus. They played board games sometimes. And a lot of the prayers were silent, so I could think about stuff."

Robin counted, in a little notebook, and when she figured out she and Terry hadn't had sex in three months, and he was too broke even to go to the movies or for anything to eat more expensive than McDonald's, she broke up with him. It meant she had to move out of their place, because she couldn't afford it by herself. She moved in with another girl who worked at the Co-op, and who was taking online university classes. Robin looked into her roommate's catalogue, but couldn't find anything she wanted to study, so she took a student loan and a class on cutting hair that cost as much as a good used car.

"Could you cut my hair?"

"Sure. But it's kind of bumpy back here. I might do a shitty job."

"Another time, then."

They just cuddled, on the way to Edmonton. Robin thought maybe David was gay, until he shifted and rubbed his hard-on against her butt. He was wearing pyjama pants, too, and she thought if he wasn't careful they'd both get wet.

He got off the bus in Snake River with his jacket tied around his waist to hide his erection. Robin thought he'd probably paid for most of the liquor, because he handed half her money back. And she was sure the coolers were just for her.

"I got some gin for myself."

Robin wrinkled her nose. "Yuck."

"Well, I'm not sharing, so don't worry about it."

They kept the bottles in their bags at the Edmonton bus station, because they wouldn't let you on the bus if they thought you were drunk. She could see why. It was downtown, and it looked like a downtown bus station. Most of the people from up north scattered. The people who got on the new bus, except for her and David, were poorer and sadder looking. A lot of old guys, and some girls who looked like they'd been hooking, or else taking meth recreationally. Not a lot of full sets of teeth. The Indian guy with the blue pillow and the box of Ritz Crackers pointedly sat by himself and listened to an old Walkman with the cheap headphones Robin remembered from when she was little.

David said, "He's gonna need a lot of batteries."

So Robin said, "I might have, too, if you hadn't invited me over." And then, because he didn't get the joke, she bounced her forefinger up and down against her crotch.

It was night. They'd be in Saskatoon sometime around dawn. Another shitty downtown station. Robin had heard that since she'd travelled through last, they'd moved the Winnipeg station out by the airport. She kept mapping out her trip in her head, over and over, trying to find her way home when she wasn't quite sure home was still where she'd put it.

David whispered, "I could do that for you."

"What?"

"I want to touch your pussy. Okay?"

So she let him. He turned so he was leaning against the wall, then pulled Robin halfway into his lap and pushed his hand down into her pants. He was under her panties' waistband so quick that he was combing her pubes before Robin could say, "I think you're supposed to kiss me first."

He pulled his hand back. When he put the same fingers on her cheek, she could smell herself. She was wet. Really obviously. He turned her face towards him. Said, "Listen."

Shit, she thought. She'd maybe blown this. Because he was really just some guy she'd met on the bus, and she did want him to touch her, but if she scared him, he might kick her out of the back seat and she'd have to take care of herself in the ladies' room of the next gas station they passed that was actually open.

"Never mind."

"No," he said. "Listen. Um. I really like you. I should've asked to kiss you first, but when you said that, *touch your pussy* was all I could think of."

"You should kiss me, then."

So they kissed, and it was a mess. Robin tried again, and it went a bit better, until he licked at her, and then she started laughing and had to push away from him. David said, "Sorry."

"No, I'm just nervous. Can I have a drink?"

He handed her one of the coolers and told her to keep it low, where no one could see it. She chugged it like a kid with a soda. The gas pressure built up just under her breastbone, and she had to bolt for the toilet to belch somewhere other than in his face. There was no real sink in there, just a hand-sanitizer dispenser. She used some of that. If anybody smelled alcohol on her, she could say it was the sanitizer. She unfolded the tiny door and went back out. David was sitting cross-legged with his back against the window; up close, he smelled like gin. When she sat down, he said, "Let me try that again," and kissed her very carefully, and hard.

Robin thought, *I can feel that in my arm hairs.*

She sat up, leaning in to kiss him, until they pulled into the next town. The bus lights were off and she could hear most of the bus people snoring. The driver got off and pulled out packages for the cargo deliveries, and Robin climbed into David's lap and kissed her way down into his mouth like she could get inside his skin like that.

He did touch her pussy, later. He'd pulled her back into his lap, and kissed her neck while he fingered her. He couldn't really get inside, but he did a better job than she expected, and the warm rush that came up through her grafted her heart onto her breastbone. Trying to get at him. Eat him up. Make him do that again.

It was dark and tight in there

— *like you* —

— *ha ha* —

but she got down on her belly and sucked him. He pulled up his pants, after, and she rinsed her mouth with root beer. Fell asleep against him and woke up hours later, in the mostly daylight, with her heart pounding and her mouth sour from the semen and sugar. David had his fingers in her hair. Out the window, she saw they were coming under a traffic overpass, and that was Saskatoon. They pulled into the old bus station, and the lights came on properly, and the driver announced — loudly, in case anyone was still asleep — that they had one hour and five minutes. The bus would leave at 7:45 a.m.

The Saskatoon bus station was awful. It was made of orange and brown seventies tile, and the seats were orange moulded plastic, and the coffee shop didn't look like it served anything human. Robin bought a couple of plastic-wrapped muffins, and then David stepped up behind her and said, "Fuck me in the bathroom?"

The ladies room was actually worse than the rest of the station. It was intensely orange and wet all over. She had to wait for this really strange, maybe-drunk — certainly drunker than Robin — lady to leave, and then this kid wanted to come in, and she might never have got the place empty, except one of the stalls with a wrecked toilet was full of cleaning stuff, so she put out a *Closed for Cleaning* sign and pulled David in under it.

She tried sucking him again, but the floor was wet and soaked into the legs of her pyjamas. She got up and threw the little bolt on the bathroom door, and just peeled off all her clothes. Her T-shirt and bra and pyjama pants and her panties all went onto the sink ledge, so she was only wearing her socks and runners. In the dirty mirror, she saw her hair all tangled and slept-on.

David said, "Oh fuck. Thank you." He bent her over the sink. He had to bend his knees a little to reach. "I'll get you off later again. Promise. Oh, thank you."

She realized he was big before she thought about the absence of a condom. She tried to speak. "Shh," he said. "Someone's going to hear." But he wouldn't stop pushing *in* like that, and just before he came, he whispered, "Pinch your nipples for me."

"I can't. I'll fall over."

"Do it later and show me."

"Yeah."

He came growling a couple of thrusts later, and pulled out right away after. Robin felt part of the wet slide away before she could reach to catch it. She braced herself to stand up. It was there, on the floor. She wasn't sure you'd know what it was if you didn't know they'd been fucking in the bathroom. She used toilet paper to clean herself up, but the floor was too wet for that, and anyway, there was no paper towel.

"I feel bad. Somebody's going to have to clean that up."

"You're not drunk enough."

It was probably true. It was probably also true that nobody cleaned there, ever, so she pulled her clothes back on, and she went out of the bathroom first, and was back on the bus long before David showed up. He'd bought a bottle of something from a guy waiting to meet his girlfriend off the bus from Regina who said he could get more, anyway, as soon as the stores opened at ten. There was no time to disguise the bottle as anything else, but David had his jacket wrapped around it, and he stuffed the whole mess onto the floor.

She sat separately, for a bit. Actually got up and took over a different pair of seats. Looked out the window. She'd bought a ticket to Winnipeg, where one of her friends lived and had a couch Robin could sleep on for a while, until she could get her own place. Winnipeg had cheaper places for rent than Cut Hand, and more room for another hairdresser. She reminded herself that David was going to Hamilton. She'd never been that far east. He'd have to go through all of northern Ontario, maybe across Manitoulin Island. There was a wall of woods and water between where she was going and where he was going.

She was tired, and partly homeless, so it felt fair that she should get to cry about this. She was prepared to be quiet about it. Just angry that the best guy she'd met in ages was headed to a place a thousand miles away from her, and if she wanted to chase him she'd have to come up with the money, quick, for another ticket, and then think of a good reason to tell him she'd — just randomly — decided to move to Ontario instead, and he shouldn't worry too much about it.

She wasn't sure he was actually going through Toronto, even. If she bought a ticket to Toronto, she could pretend she wasn't following him. Robin tried to remember if she knew anybody who was living in Toronto, right then. If she'd had her phone, she could have checked Facebook, while they were still in Saskatoon's cell range. It was dead, though. Too dead even to ask David to program his number into it for later.

It was its own kind of good feeling, this misery. Hopeless nobody-loves-me waves that she could ride for a while. They pushed back some of the sex-longing. David's body-spray smell was on her, though. When she pulled the neck of her T-shirt up to rub her face on it, she could smell him almost as much as she could smell the horrible bathroom. She needed to change clothes. The tiny bus toilet had enough room for her to do that, at least.

Her panties were sticky. She should have changed in Saskatoon, but she'd left her bag on the bus. She'd had to walk back to the bus with her pyjamas wet from the bathroom floor.

David looked asleep. She crawled in along the floor and dug through her backpack. No more pyjamas, but she had old, almost-worn-out jeans and a looser T-shirt she could wear without a bra. Getting the mess of her clothes off in the can, though, was almost impossible. She knocked the folding door open and had to grab at it. In the end, she stood absolutely straight and pulled on her pants by jumping up and down. The bus floor shook viciously under her. When she came out, David was awake and grinning.

"Sounded like you were getting it on in there all by yourself."

"I just needed new clothes."

"You look cute. Come here."

They ate her muffins, and the coolers — three left — tasted enough like juice to be called breakfast. Robin ate a handful of pretzels, and drank some root beer, and the remains of the not-Sprite vodka, and some of the bottle — it was rye — that David had cadged in Saskatoon. It pushed the crying-sad back and let her wriggle up against him. "Hey. Hey, I really like you too."

Morning on the bus was different. People got on. Old ladies in small towns climbed in and sat up front talking to the driver, then got off half an hour later. The Indian with the Ritz Crackers got off at Foam Lake, seriously kissed a girl in a windbreaker, and got into a car with her. It looked like true love, even, maybe. It looked nice.

David found another phone battery. He pulled up a *Resident Evil* movie that Robin had seen before, and it looked like nothing on the tiny screen, but he gave her one of his ear buds, and took the other, and they got under his blanket and watched. Hooted at the zombies and swapped drinks in between kisses.

A lady who'd decided to sit at the back of the bus started turning around to stare at them, near Yorkton. She gave them big, you're-making-too-much-noise, snarling glares. Shut-up-you-damn-kids. Robin decided she liked somebody calling her a *damn kid*, even silently. Like she'd erased the last two or three years of her life. She grinned at the lady. Waved.

"Shh," David hissed. "She'll want to play too!"

So she shut up, until the lady went back to her knitting, or whatever she was doing. Robin tucked her head against David's shoulder.

They finished the cadged bottle by Yorkton. David said he could cover it, and took off to find new drinks. In the Yorkton downtown, Robin wasn't sure there was even a beer store. Saskatchewan was different about liquor sales. She couldn't see anything. She got a chicken burger at the little restaurant, but it was raw inside and she didn't want to eat it.

David was a better searcher than she expected. Even so, all he found was beer.

"There was a hotel off-sale."

"What's an off-sale?"

"Where you buy takeout beer at the hotel."

"You'd think you were from here."

"I worked here for a while. A while ago. You get used to it."

"Even the flat part?"

"I thought you were from Winnipeg."

"I'm not!" Too loud. "I just know some people in Winnipeg. I'm not *from* there."

"Oh yeah? Where are you from, then?"

"Your dreams. Give me one of those." She could finish the licorice later, to cover her breath. Beer was a slow drink, anyway. "Jesus, are these cans?"

"All I could find."

She got most of the foam in her mouth, just a bit on her shirt. Pushed up into David's lap, facing him, and kissed him. Took another drink and passed it to him. Miles slid past, and for sure, she was going to put the ticket to Toronto on her Visa, and then make like she was going down to Hamilton in a few days, so he could just write her number on his arm, or something, and she'd call him up so they could hang out.

Robin didn't think she was laughing or anything, but when they pulled in at some little place, the bus driver came walking back up the aisle to them. "Hey, you two. Maybe you could keep it —" He looked at them. "Huh."

"Hey."

The driver sort of hugged himself. Looked them over. "I think maybe you guys need some air, yeah?"

Robin was a little embarrassed — not seriously, but like she'd been caught by a teacher making out in a classroom at lunch hour. Like she was going to have to take a dose of *cool it* and a temporary pause.

"We're okay."

"Come on," he said. "If you die of a blood clot back here because you stayed still too long, I'll get in trouble. Stretch your legs."

David said, "Okay." Like it was logical. He pushed Robin gently off his lap and got up. His dick was swinging against his pyjama pants. He walked down the aisle, past the grumpy old lady, towards the front stairs. The driver nodded at Robin.

"You too. You'll feel better."

They weren't really anywhere. There was a little pavilion, and the sign said they were on the Saskatchewan-Manitoba border. Tourist information, maps, points of interest. Nobody was smoking. The air was just a bit cold, left over from the night.

Robin stretched. Reached upwards and let her shirt rise to air out her navel.

Behind her, the bus driver said, "You're really drunk, I think. I can smell it from here."

"What?" She turned towards him. He'd pulled the bus doors mostly shut, and was leaning against them.

"You've been drinking for a while, and it wasn't a problem until you started disturbing the other passengers. Not to mention the other stuff." Nodding at David's pants. "So here's what we're going to do. I'm going to go back in and get your stuff. Do you have anything underneath?"

"Yeah." Numbly.

"I'll get you that, too. And when you've sobered up, you can go in there and call someone to come get you."

Robin shivered. She'd forgotten to find panties. Almost naked, in the middle of the flat nowhere at the centre of the world. She thought about what the driver had said. Working through it took a minute.

"Hang on. You're leaving us here?"

"You're being refused service."

"What? No fucking way!" David pushed up in front of her. Almost like chivalry. He was a big guy, she thought. He had muscles. She'd have to get him naked. "I paid through to Hamilton."

"And you forfeited it when you transported alcohol, opened it, and consumed it on the bus. I could've left you in Saskatoon, you were so obviously loaded, but at least you were mostly quiet."

Robin sat down. Her earlier-morning cry was pushing back up.

David was pushing closer to the bus driver. "I *paid*."

"I'm going to go get your stuff. Calm down."

"You open those doors and I'm getting back on."

"If you try, I will call the RCMP. We have a zero-tolerance policy. And you've had a lot of tolerance. A lot."

"I haven't been kicked off anything in my life."

"Dude. It's okay. You need to calm down. You're not getting back on the bus." Pause. "Either of you."

David turned back to Robin. She waited. Waited for him to at least make a case for her. Like, she'd behave. Without him, she'd be no problem. And then, at least, she could announce she wasn't going to get back on by her lonesome, and the driver could fuck himself.

There was a knock. The grumpy lady stood at the bus doors with Robin's stuff in her arms. The driver pulled the doors open a little and took the clumped-up mess from her. Grumpy reached back up the stairs and pushed David's bag and sleeping stuff out onto the gravel.

Robin's bag had been open when Grumpy threw it, and now her sticky pyjamas and layers of her underwear were spilling out into the little parking lot. Wind pushed at them. She was going to have to get up, rescue her things before they got carried away into the brush or into the big falling-away fields past that. The neckline of her T-shirt gaped as she stood. She tried to decide if the bus driver was looking. Grumpy could see, but she'd already decided Robin was naked before God, and losing her shirt was just par for the course.

Her panties caught on a prickly branch. Rose bush, a big one. She tugged, trying to get them loose. The bus driver, distantly, said, "You should probably help her."

"Dude, come on."

Robin came back with her underwear, and David was crying. Trying to get close enough to the bus driver that he could — what? Hug him? Apologize? Steal his keys?

"You can't get back on. When you sober up, you can call your friends or call the cops."

He got their bags for them, but didn't pass them over. Just left them piled in the dirt, and got into the bus carefully, like he was trying to keep cats from escaping, and once he was sure that David wasn't under the tires, he drove away.

Robin went to step up behind David, maybe to hug him. He shrugged her off. She felt his chest shake under her hands, before he got loose, and she realized he was crying. He was making the deep-bone, high crying sound she associated with kids and death. He bolted away from her, towards the pavilion and tugged at the door. It was locked.

She listened while he screamed at the sky. He swore, but not in the kind of detail she could remember, after. Just a constant, pounding *fuck, fuck, fuck*.

The wind pushed against the clothes Robin stuffed into her bag. When David didn't come back, she gathered up his bedding and pulled it into the shelter of the trees. His phone was there, too, but it had no signal. None of the batteries he had would fit her phone at all. Anyway, she needed to sleep. No idea what she was going to do, and if she kept standing, she was going to get dizzy, and then maybe throw up.

David's blanket was an old comforter. It made a terrible sleeping bag, but she was too tired to get extra clothes to make it softer. She fell asleep with her head on her backpack, woke up later and peed in the trees because the pavilion was still locked. She noticed, numbly, that there was an outside payphone. Later. She went back to the mess of a bed.

It wasn't winter, at least. The leaves were down, but they smelled good, and the wind sounded like a real, outdoorsy thing. She drifted, not really asleep, and eventually she felt David crawl in behind her and wrap his whole body around hers, holding her down with his arm and leg.

Sometime after, the police came. Like maybe the bus driver had had the decency to tell them he'd abandoned a couple of people on the edge of the world.

They drove Robin and David in the back of the car to Russel, in Manitoba. They had to hold their bags with them in the back, packed in like a third world trip of some sort. The police booked them and issued disorderly fines, then let them go. Took note of Robin's driver's license, and David's.

"How am I supposed to get out of here?" David asked.

"The bus guys don't want you," the constable told him. "I wouldn't be surprised if you find yourself permanently banned."

"They don't know who I am."

"You gave them your name when you bought your ticket. Also, I bet it's on your luggage."

"Shit. How am I supposed to get home?"

"Your problem. I guess you could hire a cab."

"All the way to Ontario?"

Shrug.

Robin had been standing behind David all day. He was shaking angrily, and now closer to hungover than drunk. His back was hunched, and she wondered if he was younger than she was. How much?

She said, "If you can get to Winnipeg, you can stay with my friends." Pause. "You can stay at my place. Until. Whatever. There's a train station."

David turned to look at her. "Split the cab?"

Part of Robin's brain screamed that only Indians took taxis that far. That he had more money than she did.

She nodded.

The cab driver who came to the RCMP detachment said he didn't care what they did as long as they didn't have open liquor in the car and didn't fuck where he could see them. He loaded their bags for them carefully, like it was a special service. Got in, guarded by his scratched bulletproof shield, and turned onto the highway.

It took more than six hours. When David hadn't said anything, she'd asked the driver for a flat rate, and he'd told her

$250. He thought maybe he could get a fare on the way back, so she wouldn't have to pay him for the other way. She said, "I only have a credit card."

"You sort that out between you."

David slept on the other side of the car until Minnedosa. Then he reached out for Robin. The driver glanced in the rearview. He said, "Keep your seat belts on, please."

David took Robin's hand. Stroked its palm and kissed it. Held it all the rest of the way, while her shoulder slowly stiffened. She could feel his pulse in her half-numb fingers.

At the Perimeter Highway in Winnipeg, the driver asked her for an address. Robin's phone was still dead. She had to dig in her bag, looking for scraps of paper with useful information.

She'd forgotten how to navigate the city. Couldn't figure out where they were going. The driver had turned his metre back on at the city limits, when he activated his GPS, and she realized he was going to bill them extra for the city miles.

In the dry residential half-dark, Robin had to push David awake. She said, "Can you use your credit card?"

He stared at her.

"I'll pay you back in the morning," she said. "Only. I don't think I can cover the whole thing."

He paid the guy. Asked for a receipt, and didn't tip. It meant David had to lift his own bags out of the trunk, and Robin had to get hers. She had to drag them up the dark sidewalk to what she hoped was still Nadine's side door.

When she opened up — and it wasn't right away, long enough to make Robin think about what time it was — Nadine stared at both of them. "I thought you weren't coming."

"We had an accident."

"Who's this?"

"He's David."

"Christ, where'd you find him?"

"If I tell you in the morning, can I keep him?"

Nadine let Robin in. To David, she said, "Stay there." Like he'd go wandering off and steal her city-issued curbside rubbish bins.

"You can't stay here with him."

"Hi," said Robin. "I missed you."

"I missed you too. But you can't stay here with him."

"Let me keep him until morning."

"Did you marry him or something?"

"Not yet."

Nadine studied Robin through mostly closed eyes. She was wearing a T-shirt nightie. She swayed. Asleep standing. Robin stared longer.

Nadine's husband staggered out in his underpants. "What?"

"I think she went back to sleep," Robin said.

"Damn. Can you put yourself to bed? We left some blankets in the basement. Lock the door, yeah?" He walked Nadine back to bed. Over his shoulder, "See you in the morning."

Robin waited until there was no creaking. Then she let David in.

The basement wasn't finished. They'd blown up an air mattress and left some sheets and an old, light blanket on it. One pillow. Robin showered in the tiny stall in the laundry room. Because it was all she could find, she used body wash for shampoo. She came out with tangled hair, shivering. David had curled up still stinking on the bed. He took up most of the mattress, but when she knelt to work her way in, he opened his body up and tangled into her. Whispered, "I like you *so much.*"

Robin whispered, "I like you too."

Later, she realized they'd left his bags outside. There were leaves in his hair. Nadine's cat came down the stairs, shit in its box, and crawled into bed with them. Robin reached out to her bag and found half a warm root beer. She drank it. Thought about how, if she had to pee, she'd have to get loose from both animals holding her down. Her phone wasn't plugged in. David's was there, though, on the floor. She caught it with her fingertips and flipped it open. Facebook gave up a list of Winnipeg-based names to her. These people she'd been friends with who'd gotten married while she was away and bought houses. She keyed messages to them carefully, using just her thumb. Whispered requests for shelter. Two people. Not taking up much room.

Any corner would do. They'd be positively cozy.

The Witch Invites
Herself to Dinner

MY MOTHER IS AN APPALLING WITCH. FOR THIS reason, and others, she lives in a Vancouver rental, and I live in Winnipeg like a grown woman with a life of her own and we don't talk much. She sends me complicated Christmas letters and I send her a card, and about one year in three she sends me something strange for my birthday, like bags of unground spices from this Indian place on Commercial Drive, or a bunch of paperclips and loose change that she picked up in a parking lot while she was thinking of me. It says so on the scrap of paper she sticks in with it.

She sends me letters written in what I eventually determined was blackberry juice. It wasn't red enough to be blood, but the writing was smeared. I thought it might be some sort of threat. The letter was about what books she'd borrowed from the library, and what she thought of them. Just random books. I couldn't even have made out her taste from the list.

She sends me teeth.

She sent me the first ones when I was twenty-six, all

together in a plastic sandwich bag. They were tiny and flat, and she said they were mine. I wouldn't have bet on that. All the teeth I remember losing, I lost after I went to live with Frank and Bernadette, and we dutifully sacrificed them to the tooth fairy.

Each tooth went into a green plastic cup of water. The cup is oddly stylish, in my memory. It came from Ikea, back when Ikea was a pretty cool idea. It was vaguely hippy-ish, but less so than anything I had been exposed to by my mother. In comparison to her, Ikea was just *relaxed*. Calm about the possibilities that might leap out of a house on any given Thursday.

Frank and Bernadette had plastic cups because Aimee was a toddler then, and James was eight months, and they wanted plastic dishes until everyone got old enough to hold a glass without shattering it. I'd mostly drunk out of old mugs, up to that point. The green cups seemed impossibly glamorous. Almost magical.

We used plastic cups for the teeth. Bernadette said that the West Coast tooth fairy was aquatic. She liked diving. The coastal tooth fairies practiced on fish teeth, down at the bottom of Burrard Inlet. I remember I was worried about that, because we'd filled the cup with tap water, and it wasn't the same. So Bernadette got the salt shaker, and Frank brought in some rock salts he'd collected in university, when he thought he might be a geologist, and we made sea water very, very carefully. The tooth fairy collected each of my teeth and gave me quarters.

My first lost molar earned an actual post-silver silver dollar. Frank collected them. It was really sweet of him.

Retrospect.

When my mother sent me the bag of teeth, I called Bernadette to ask. My early memory isn't entirely reliable. She said she'd check, if it made me feel better.

"Hang on, baby." I waited on the phone while she walked upstairs, and then while she rummaged in her jewellry box. My fairy teeth were in there, along with her and Frank's two kids', each set in a velvet ring box. She counted them.

"We're short three for you. How many did she send?"

She'd sent me eight. I told Bernadette, "Eleven."

Bernadette said, "Do you want me to talk to her?"

My mother's shed a dozen skins, but when I was a teenager she alternated between looking like a mad, badly addicted street person and a depressive divorcee. Bernadette looks like a very Canadianized family lawyer with the faintest hint of Cantonese in her CBC English. From her grandmother, who insisted Bernadette go to Chinese school after regular school.

She's more Canadian than I am. They've been here five generations. I can only guarantee three, and that's assuming my mother didn't fall to earth from some other dimension early in the Second World War, when everyone was too distracted to notice. Bernadette looked more normal than I did, walking me down East Pender in 1983. She took me to see my mom on alternate Saturday afternoons. Regular, like swimming lessons, which my visits with her prevented me from ever having.

€ € €

I swim these days at the Pan-Am pool, twice a week after work and once on the weekend, Saturday or Sunday, whichever I have time for. During the week, Ellie meets me there when she's finished school. I've been coaxing her to swim, but she's going through a period when she can't stand to be seen in public in a bathing suit. At the beach, she wears huge T-shirts over her one-piece, and when she comes out of the water, she looks like a woman who drowned in her pyjamas.

I buy her suits. I don't know how well they fit, because she won't let me see her wear them. Bernadette reminds me that I should try to surprise Ellie from time to time while she's changing clothes or showering, just to make sure she's not cutting herself, or anything like that. Girls do that, now. Girls did that when I was her age, too, but we thought it was a personal invention. Every cutter I ever met thought she'd invented the practice. Now they learn about it in special web forums, I suppose. There are probably web communities just for cutters.

I know there are. Girls take headless pictures of themselves and show off the damage. Boys too.

I was surprised at how sexy I found the boys' pictures. Shocked. Shocked with myself, because I'm fairly sure there's a jurisdiction where that qualifies as child pornography, and because I'm old enough to be their mother. Still. My thing for sad, broken boys never goes away.

Bernadette likes Brendan. My mother doesn't. She kept tabs on me, even after I fled Vancouver, and once she sent me a letter telling me not to marry no poets. I never did take her advice. Look at the state of her. Why would I?

Brendan's penchant for self-mutilation these days is mostly limited to long-distance running. I buy him decent shoes and hope his bones won't break.

Ellie won't run with her dad, either. She rides the stationary bike we have set up in the basement, but only when no one else is present. She watches streaming episodes of TV down there, and I suppose it's safe enough. I checked her viewing list, and there's nothing too obscene. Teenagers' dramas, mostly.

She watches the pornographic show about vampires in

pirated files on her dad's computer. If he wants to have that conversation with her, he's welcome.

Ellie walks over to the Pan-Am complex from school and sits in the massive stands above the main pool while I swim. At that hour, only the massive open pool is available for public use. I have to fight the cross-currents of other swimmers, and occasionally I'm struck by the shockwave of someone hitting the water in a botched dive. It's harder work than lane swimming; I tell myself this is good for me. Better exercise, and lessons in determination for dealing with teenagers and the looming threat of the witch of the West Coast, who's been sending me notes asking if I have a few dollars for her gas bill.

The thing is, I pay her gas bill every month. Electric too. I set it up so they just come to me electronically. Brendan knows. We send his parents money from time to time. Ellie doesn't know, because I told her we couldn't cover the insurance for her to have a car. She can use mine, once a week.

My mother, thank god, doesn't drive. My mother is going to lose it one of these days and I can only hope she doesn't use the gas I'm paying for to blow up her house and take out the neighbours.

€ € €

My mother has been collecting teeth since at least 1962, when she got a job in a dentist's office in Cache Creek, BC, and he enlisted her as a hygienist-assistant.

In those days, there was no program for licensing hygienists. You didn't have to be a trained technician, any more than you had to be a nurse to work at the hospital, and even the nurses were just girls with a few months on-the-job training and strong stomachs. Dentists probably weren't even regulated. The dentist was, I think, legitimately trained, though he'd come over as a Hungarian refugee and didn't speak a huge amount of English. My mother was his public face. She was born up there, in the high interior, and she had a local accent, tightly sprayed hair, and a nice smile. You could trust a girl like that. I've seen a couple of photos, and I'd probably have trusted her too.

She married Frank in 1963. Poor Frank. He was doing survey work up there for logging companies, and she looked so… normal. Like a wife. He was the kind of man who wanted a wife. All the guys had wives. They had babies and pushed carriages and made meatloaf.

He must have thought it was weird that she wouldn't stop working for the dentist. What he said to me, later, was that she said they needed the money. They could get a house faster, and a better car. And the dentist wouldn't mind. He'd love it that his nurse-receptionist was a "Mrs." It was more respectable. A matron. Practically medical herself.

So Frank moved with the lumber companies around the north of the province. He went on fly-in surveys. Eventually, he was hired by a mining company, and some weeks he had to go up to the uranium mines on the territorial border. My mother stayed by herself in Cache Creek, being the next best thing to the dentist.

They didn't have biohazardous waste rules in those days. They probably burned bloody cloths, but everything else just went in the trash unless people specifically asked for it. At the hospital, if they took out a little extra organ, they'd stick it in a jar for you to appreciate. A curio. Put it up on the mantel next to the taxidermied heads. *Oh that? They dug it out of me up north. Called it an appendix. Thought I'd keep it as a memento. No shit.*

Kids wanted their teeth for the fairy, of course, but adults mostly didn't care. They didn't just have one tooth out in those days: they'd come in and have them all out at once. Get it over with. Gum it or get dentures. At the end of a day the office must have had enamel kidney trays full of bloody, half-rotted teeth. The dentist left clean-up to my mother.

She was hygienic. I have to give her that. She soaked each set in alcohol for a week before she dried them off for storage. In the early days, I think she kept the teeth together in sets. It must have had a voodoo effect, power over each individual person, and she'd known them all her life. A little something for private revenge, a little sympathetic magic, held in reserve for the right moment.

Later, she started sorting them by type. Left lower bicuspid. Dozens of them in a jam jar at the back of the cupboard. Frank found them, probably three or four years in. He wasn't a guy to make his own lunch in those days. I always picture him staring at the jars like he thought they might be one of the mysterious ingredients in his sandwiches. Seasonings for the soup? Some new legume she was experimenting with?

Maybe she just wanted some adventure. They took a vacation down to San Francisco. My mother took off. Left Frank in the hotel room and never came back. She must have loved the city, like she'd found the people she was always looking for. In 1969, Frank tracked her down and filed for divorce in the States, where it was easier. She didn't ask for anything. She was living in a commune in the New Mexico desert, and probably told him that words on paper couldn't bind her, and he was welcome to be as free as she was.

Frank threw away the teeth when he cleaned out their Cache Creek apartment and moved to northern Saskatchewan full time.

My mother started her next collection while she was in the desert. It's best not to ask her where those came from, because she'll tell you all about it.

€ € €

When they apprehended me in 1974, we were living outside Kelowna. I like the word *apprehended*. It has all these criminal overtones, but I like its sonic association with *comprehended*. Discovery of Alana! She is four years old, wearing a T-shirt and no panties, and sitting in a bush. The hippies have been arrested! They are growing things. Mysterious things. One of them is collecting teeth. Don't ask about that. You don't want to know.

It was how I met Frank. He drove out from Vancouver, where he was living by then, and met me very formally in the welfare office. In 1974, Frank wore hexagonal glasses like he thought they might give him magical powers, but they were dampened by his utterly square suit and his angle-striped tie. He looked like what you think a dad should have looked like in 1974. He was married again, with two little kids, and he'd driven all night.

I have no memory of this. I don't think even Ellie has clear memories of when she was four, and she's had a full photographic record to rely on. I only have Frank's (sketchy) details and Bernadette's better ones, but Bernadette was absent from that first encounter. Her version of things is that I shook Frank's hand. I was wearing an old-fashioned little-girl dress with bloomers, and Mary Jane shoes. I wonder if I'd ever had shoes before. He said, *I'm going to be your dad for a while. Because I know your mom. Okay?*

I went to live with Frank and Bernadette in Kitsilano. Frank said I'd make a great sister for his kids. Like I'd make a great playhouse. A slide. But what did I know?

Bernadette calls Frank *your dad* when she talks about him.

He never did that to her, call her *your mom,* but they seemed decided on terms by the time I showed up. They were living in this big old house, the kind that you could get easily then — if you were an engineer and a lawyer, certainly — and that nobody can get now. They'd done it up with a few hippy gestures that I do remember. There were macrame plant hangers, and some abstract art on the walls. Big potted house plants. There was a massive garden in the back, though the front of the house was aggressively normal-looking. They had a nice lawn. The neighbours probably wanted that, if they were going to put up with the Chinese lady living there.

After Frank died, Bernadette went to sell the house, but she said she saw the real estate prices and almost died. Decided she couldn't deal with those sums of money and just went on living there. She got a couple of roommates, and then she converted the house into apartments and went to live upstairs. I told her to do what she wanted. Anyway, money from the house goes to Aimee and James. It's fair: she's their mother. She and Frank sent me to university, and they gave me some money to get set up when I said I had to leave Vancouver, because *she* wasn't going anywhere.

€ € €

I make Ellie come out to Vancouver with me. She's been before, when she was little. I'd take her out to see Bernadette and Frank, and we'd go up to the University of British Columbia campus to see the art. And then Ellie would get bored and lie down on the floor of the gallery and I'd have to carry her out and leave her with Frank for the afternoon. Go down to the other side of the city and deal with my mother on my own. Bernadette had a deal with me. She'd call, from her office, after two hours, or have one of the paralegals do it, and that was my signal to get out.

My mother talked one of those paralegals into coming down for a psychic reading. At the time she had a whole series of clients who were divorced women in their fifties looking for something really *real*. My mother must have looked like she qualified. She went silver early, and she lived in this old row house full of dried herbs, and in her living room none of the furniture had legs. You had to fold yourself down onto the cushions at floor level and sit cross-legged.

She had good taste in incense. Somebody brought this amazing clove stuff over from Korea for her, and it was the only thing of hers I ever wanted to steal.

Ellie and my mother did not meet. Ellie knows that I have a mother, and that she's pretty strange, and that Frank and Bernadette are her "real" grandparents.

On the plane, Ellie plays complex pattern games on her phone and nibbles on M&Ms out of the bulk bag I bought her at Walmart on our way to the airport. She ignores the book I stuffed in there next to the chocolate. Just a suggestion. I have a list of good places to take her to in Vancouver. Bookstores. She knows the Winnipeg McNally Robinson, it's only a stone's throw from her high school, but it lacks the thrill of the exotic. We can go shopping on South Granville, and I'll take her to Gastown and buy her one really nice thing. She has a taste for East Asian stuff that I think must be inspired by the anime shows she watches, and I'm considering whether to drive her out to Surrey for one of the night markets.

All the interesting girls run away to Vancouver as soon as they can. I'm not sure yet whether Ellie intends to be *interesting*, but it doesn't hurt to give her ideas. I'll float her tuition at UBC if she really wants to go.

I had no intention of taking her to see my mother, but I should have expected that that wouldn't work. I'm asleep on the guest futon at Bernadette's, and Ellie's curled up on the window-seat couch, when my cell rings and it's — no kidding — the police. I am, unexpectedly, my mother's emergency contact. Her place was broken into, probably by junkies, but they found teeth in jars all over the house, and called the police themselves, and in the meantime my mother slipped in the dark and cut her head on the broken glass and, please, can I come and get her?

Ellie says, "Who's dead?"

"Sadly, not my mom. Shit. Sorry. Forget I said that." I have a rule that I don't complain about her in front of Ellie. There are versions of things she doesn't have to be embedded in.

"Is she okay?"

"I don't know. I have to go. Go back to sleep."

Instead, she turns on the light. She's wearing pyjama pants and a T-shirt, but she skins the pants off and goes looking for panties out of her bag. I stare at her backside like I'm ogling. There are no clear razor cuts, but there are shallowly bruised places like she's been digging with her nails. Information for later. "I want a Tim's coffee on the way over," she tells me. Just like she's coming along.

I make her stay. Or, I make Bernadette make her stay. I have to promise I'll bring back coffee and Timbits for breakfast. I'm so cold. I woke up cold, and I shake hard all the way across the city. In the small hours of Tuesday, Vancouver's party scene is dead or shifted up to Whistler, where they party like it's West Berlin and the end of the world. There are cold-looking girls walking the streets, but I don't feel as bad for them as I do for me. The blasting car heater doesn't help enough. I need to sleep. Even in the hospital lobby, it occurs to me just to curl up on the plastic seats and sleep for a couple of hours. A woman balefully throws her coat over two extra seats when I lean in her direction, just to keep me away.

There's a social worker sitting with my mother, and some-one from what I'm informed is Victim Services, and also a police officer. They can't decide, I think, whether she's dangerous or needing to be saved. Whether to charge her or make her supper. She has stitches under her eye. In a few hours, it'll be a classic shiner.

I say, "What would you have done if I hadn't been in town?"

"I knew you were here."

"Bernadette told you."

"I scried for it. I always know where you are."

❦ ❦ ❦

I take her with me, but I can't take her home. They want to have a forensic team go over her place in the morning. I take her to a Denny's in Burnaby, just so we can be out of everyone's territory, and stare at her.

"Do you have friends you can stay with?"

"Call Bernadette."

"No. I'll get you a motel room."

She picks at her chicken fingers and mixed peas and corn. Her giant strawberry lemonade looms obscenely neon between us. I ordered for her. She used to do that for me, in Chinatown when Bernadette left me with my mother for the afternoon, and she insisted that I eat what I was served carefully, with chop-sticks.

Bernadette lets me use a fork.

And I don't. Try again.

My phone buzzes. Ellie.

U ok

I'm fine. Back for breakfast. Love you.

Ellie's inventory of my failings includes my need to use punctuation when texting. She hasn't yet discovered that it self-generates if you just space things out, and that the capitalization is automatic.

I have them put the lemonade into a takeout cup, and we drive around until daylight. It's raining, and I have to pull into a parking lot to tell Ellie that I'll be a couple of hours yet. Waiting. My mother dozes. I was right about the black eye; she looks like an elderly battered wife, one of those women without the brains or courage to get out during the first forty years of a bad marriage.

It occurs to me that I could take her to a shelter. A women's shelter, not a homeless shelter. The homeless don't need to be afflicted with her. But if any of the women's shelters are still being run by the old hippies, they might just love her. She can cook their lentil soups and tell the fortunes of scared girls until she thinks of what she's going to do next.

My phone has some web access, but not enough for full search capabilities. The public libraries won't open for hours. I desperately need sleep.

I take her home. Home, I mean, to her house. The police are there, but they look finished. People with white-baggied feet carefully step out.

They take my mother with them for questioning. I don't offer to go along.

It's the teeth. Her house is full of jars of teeth. I don't suppose any of them are original to the ancient Hungarian dentist's practice, but she's clearly developed other suppliers. A few jars are obviously missing: the forensic investigators have taken them for careful dental autopsies.

I clean up. The glass sweeps away as easily as a broken cup, and there are garbage bags under the sink for me to tape over the gaping hole where the bathroom window used to be. Otherwise, my mother's bathroom is neat. The wall is hung with a pegboard supporting secondhand jewellry and a few polyester scarves. There's makeup in the medicine cabinet, though it isn't fresh and some of its colours are odd. I suspect she bought it at garage sales.

The kitchen contains a vast range of jars. There are the jars of unconfiscated teeth, high in the cupboards, but there are other jars, too. Spices and dried fruits and bits of plants. Some of those jars are missing, too, leaving lacunae in the dust on their shelves. Taken, I suppose, for substance testing.

The police missed the massive jar of dried, obvious mushrooms tucked in next to the stove vent. I stare at it.

I don't know if she's dealing. She's made her money in a lot of ways, including — though I can't prove it — back-room dentistry. The mortar-and-pestle sets around the kitchen suggest she's currently engaged in something more like herbal witchcraft. In Vancouver, there's always a market. She'd do better in the Gulf Islands, but she burned some bridges out there when I was a teenager. Urban back-door herbalist is probably, at this stage, her best option.

I wonder if she really has been grinding up teeth for nefarious purposes. Whether she's been using discarded eyelashes in secondhand makeup for low-grade spells to help civil servants find autumnal romance.

€ € €

Ellie finds the mushrooms in my purse and palms a dozen or so before I notice. She won't read the books I give her, but she reads

New Yorkers from Bernadette's bathroom. They went out for breakfast to one of the little bakeries Frank used to like. Came back to find me asleep on the futon and my purse gaping open. I'd missed two calls. Bernadette took Ellie with her to collect my mother from the police station. I didn't even wake up.

I roll over on the futon in mid-afternoon and find a headache brewing between my eyes. While I'm staggering, trying to deal with the old-fashioned latch on the bathroom door, I hear my mother's voice. It's unexpected enough that I think at first my ears are ringing. Tinnitus at the most irritating of all possible frequencies. I sit on the toilet with my panties around somewhat hairy ankles and consider my options for never coming out of the bathroom at all. I wonder what I thought would happen.

My favourite fantasy is of putting my mother into care. The fantasy skips the process of proving that she's insane or incompetent, the months or years of hearings involved. I get to swoop in, sign the necessary papers, and reclaim Vancouver. She settled in the Lower Mainland and I fled. I want it back.

I want to swim in the ocean on a regular basis. The old Kitsilano pool is gone, and I'm aware that the sea's impossibly cold, but whenever I see pictures of Vancouver, I want to jump into the water. I want to have stayed and become the kind of woman who gets to spend her whole life in the Pacific urban archipelago, loving complex teas and secondhand clothes.

I could, maybe, drown myself in the bathtub.

Ellie gets it from me. I blame her dad, but she gets it from me.

When I pull my feet back under myself and step out, Ellie's drinking dark herbal tea at Bernadette's table with my mother. I have no pants. I walk past with all the wide-assed dignity I can muster. This apartment is so tiny; when I was a kid, it was the playroom and guest room together.

While I'm dressing, I notice the missing shrooms. They're in Ellie's bag, near the top, even. If I take them, she'll know I've been snooping. If I leave them, she'll likely be seized at the airport when I drag her home.

Drag being the operative word. Ellie is talking to my mother with more engagement than she's offered me in years.

Bernadette hands me a coffee and goes back to her magazine, just like she thinks I have a good idea of how to conduct myself with this many of the women in my life locked into a single room. I can't even bring myself to sit down. So I pace. Back to the living room, back to the kitchen, back to the living room. I dig out my almost-dead cell and call Brendan.

"She's here," I say.

"Hello, love. Yeah, Ellie told me."

"What did you tell her?"

"I asked her not to push your buttons."

I drink my coffee and let my silence pour down the phone. No wire connecting us, but he has an ear for my levels of aggravation. "How are you doing?" I ask.

"How are *you* doing?"

"I'm hiding from my mother. I want her to leave Ellie alone."

"Have you told Bernadette you're worried?"

"She knows."

"Okay," he says. "Take care."

In the kitchen, I say, "What are they going to find? I mean, when they finish processing the stuff from your kitchen?"

"Teeth."

"Anything else?"

She hesitates. "I don't know quite what they took."

"Drugs?"

"Not based on the contents of your purse."

Ellie smirks at me. For an only child, she has a marvellous

grasp of the *you've been told* expression I used to turn on James and Aimee.

"Anything else?"

Bernadette says, "She's talked to me about it. I'm going to deal with it, if things come to that."

"Deal with *what*?"

"Grandma had some fingers, but she got them without killing anybody. Bernadette says they can prove it. So *relax*, Mom, okay?"

⋘ ⋘ ⋘

The fingers in question are bones. Metatarsals. They were in jars next to the teeth, and I'd probably have thought they were bird bones. In fact, she found the first two beachcombing up north. They're etched with salt. She's not, as it happens, allowed to keep those, but possessing them isn't a crime. She gives a careful account of which island, and when, and the bones are carefully returned to the Haisla nation whence they came.

Other fingers were much newer. They were mostly bone, but there were flesh traces on them. Cooked off.

"Please tell me."

"It's the easiest way to clean them."

Because they were, to be clear, medical waste. People who lost fingers for one reason or another (diabetes, cooking accidents, nighttime in East Vancouver) brought them to my mother for safekeeping. They should have gone into a hospital incinerator. Therein lies the real tale, and apparently the real crime. A man who was responsible for transporting medical waste to the incinerator got the idea of selling severed parts back to their original owners. They don't let you take your appendix home in a jar anymore, but people still want to. So he got a supply of mason jars and formaldehyde (also illegal) and started packaging body bits to order.

The junkies who haunt my mother's neighbourhood are marked by missing pieces. They'd guard their jars for a week or two, and then get high and nearly drink off the liquid, and panic.

She gave each one a home. Two years she kept the jars and their chemical washes.

"But the thing is, it's *badly* carcinogenic."

"So you *stewed* them."

This is the stuff that makes careers in investigative reporting. Thus, until my mother's court date, twenty months still in the future, Bernadette suggests I take her to Winnipeg with me. As long as she has an established address, my mother won't be considered a flight risk.

"Explain this to me."

"Alana."

Bernadette doesn't look good, actually. Worse than my mother, who has the eerie health of the worst sixties survivors.

"She and I won't get along," Bernadette says. "And if she doesn't stay with you, she has to stay with me."

It isn't fair to ask it of her. My mother's welfare rent supplement wouldn't cover the cost of any of the tiny apartments our house has been carved into, and I don't put it past Bernadette to poison my mother some night, if they're left alone in the same space. They should not be left alone together.

I say, "I'm sorry I keep tying you to her."

"It's not your fault."

"Well."

"You can blame Frank. Only he would manage to get a woman pregnant while he was serving her divorce papers."

I have a fantasy that it's Bernadette I take home with me. She installs herself in the basement suite and grows unexpectedly healthy spider plants, and tracks a path to the Fort Garry Library. I come home from work to find Ellie lying on the couch watching APTN with her. They talk about languages and colonial patterns in Canadian law.

They look at different university calendars together. The same calendars that get thrown in damp piles in the laundry room when I try to leave them, shiny and enticing, around the house.

I think Bernadette is a better mother than I am. She can even put up with children who aren't hers, and she never tried to drown me once.

I turned into my mother. I wouldn't have bet it was possible. I made an *effort* not to go that way. Instead of jars, I have lists of details. I have the inventory of my mother's house while I was cleaning it. I have a list of two hundred visits in six years while I was a teenager.

I want all those fragments back. I want to know which teeth are mine, and which father, and what happened in those first four invisible years of my life. I wonder, still, about the dentist, whether it was him.

I know Ellie is cutting herself, because the garbage can is full of cotton pads soaked with very clean lines of blood. The pads are ones I bought to remove makeup with. I don't know what instrument she's using. I've counted the paring knives. I don't think any of the house scissors are sharp enough. On the Internet, the girls who blog about cutting seem to favour box cutters. I've searched Ellie's room without finding one.

I don't want her to be so unhappy. I don't know what's wrong.

If I take my mother home, I'll never be able to extricate Ellie from the tangle of her. Even in Vancouver, they're growing into one another. They take over my futon in the living room and nap there together in the afternoon, and I'm relegated to the window seat. Bernadette retreats to her bedroom. I suspect she's barricaded the door with a chair against us.

Take your mother and go. Please.

Stress brings on my period. I wasn't expecting it for two or three days. At this stage, I'm not sure how many more I'll get. Some women hit menopause in their mid-forties. It's hereditary.

The blood on the toilet paper isn't exactly a surprise. It makes me think, though. Bernadette's bathroom is so clean. I drip almost immediately on the white tile and have to wipe it up. Two pieces of toilet paper.

I fetch a zip-lock bag from the kitchen. The two pieces go into it. In the medicine cabinet, I find nail scissors, use them to cut the split ends off my hair and the sharp tips from my toe-nails. I bite enamelled tips off my fingers. Hair from my legs. Pubic hair.

At home I've got teeth. I have Ellie's blood on cotton, in a plastic vegetable bag in my underwear drawer until I figure out what to do about it.

I book a ticket for my mother on the phone, sitting on the bathroom floor. Two bags, I tell them. Three seats together, if you can.

I can't let her sit alone with Ellie, and I don't want to leave Ellie by herself. Later, when we're back in Winnipeg, I'll find a solution. I could coax my mother out into the deepest part of the Pan-Am pool and find out whether she ever learned to swim herself. I can bury pieces of her in the garden until her spirit takes the hint.

She might just freeze to death.

They might lock her up, finally, at the end of this purgatory.

In the shower drain, there's a mix of silver and black hair. Bernadette's individual hairs are very thick. I fish a few out with a Q-tip and add them to another bag. Rolled together, all sealed, the bags look almost empty. They fit under my used underwear and the T-shirt I wore through the icy night while I went to find her. The mushrooms I gather up carefully. None left in Ellie's bag. None left in mine.

Down the hall, there's a little balcony with a chair on it, where the other residents have been sitting outside smoking. It's raining, again. I miss the rain all the time. When I'm outside in Vancouver, the light's never quite as bright as the prairies, and the humidity makes me feel like I'm under water.

How Clean Is Your House

ERIN KNOWS ABOUT SERENITY BECAUSE SHE HAD A boyfriend for a while who was in AA. He collected mirror-bevelled stickers with classic slogans on them. They covered his fridge. *One Day at a Time. Lord, grant me the serenity.*

He'd been a binge drinker in his first year of university, and his aunt had dragged him to meetings, and later he got into yoga. Skinny guy. Big curly hair. Erin would let herself into his place and he'd be standing on his head against the wall, listening to what might actually have been sitar music. So she'd sit down in front of him and look at him, upright eyes into his upside down ones, until he was finished. And then he'd fold them both down onto the futon mattress in a corner where he slept. He'd kiss her all over, using his tongue in long trails. He smelled like patchouli and he was rigorously straight-edge, but he was sweet, and he taught her about letting go, without God. Just breathe out. Empty your mind.

They didn't exactly break up. Instead, he just picked up one day and left. Moved to a little town outside Portland, the Portland in Oregon, in the wet, pretty Pacific Northwest, and ran a daycare. Then he started a small grow-op. It turned into a big one. Not that he smokes it himself — he sends her pictures of the straight-edge tattoos he's acquired, that make him look like an eighteen-year-old militant Christian — but it's clean, organic farming, and he understands needing that softened world, the one without edges that most people find only by smoking up.

The House & Garden Channel does that for Erin. Takes the edges off of things. It's almost — utopian? Yes. It's utopian. This perfect world where the floors are clean all the time and people come over for dinner carrying red wine and admire your decorating skills.

Only later, she finds out, there are shows coming in from the UK about people who have house *problems*. Homemaking equivalents of intravenous drug problems. You can't tell, really, until they roll up their sleeves and show you, but then you can't believe anyone can live like that. There are multigenerational rats in the attic. Complex mold colonies in the potting shed. Their dead parents' furniture clogs up the front room.

That last one gets her: the messes. The people who lost it for a while, who were sick or taking care of someone or depressed, who stopped picking things up at all. And their houses — they actually do have houses, mostly, not just sad little poverty apartments — get worse and worse, until the public health authorities come in and give them a choice: clean up or they'll take you down to your foundation bricks. After that, the ladies come. These big, loud women who are nothing like social workers, they come in with bags of organic cleaning products, throw away ninety percent of the contents of the house, take bacterial swabs, and put people's lives back together for them, chewing them out all the while. No sympathy. Nothing like the over-intense empathy of a social worker, the *I feel your pain* expression. Not the bitter, jaded look either. They sound like mothers — not Erin's, but other girls' mothers from when she'd been a kid, who showed up in the middle of playdates and made both Erin and her friend do chores. They had no time for your shit. Clean it up. Throw it away.

You can do it. See? Now it's nice in here.

€ € €

Serenity helps, when you spend your day awash in children. Grade threes are forces of entropy, and they create mess on a scale that might daunt even the English cleaning ladies. Erin can deal with that. She's less sure how to address the deep, universal imbalance of an evangelical parent who wonders if Erin will please, *please* come with them to church for a few Sundays.

Their daughter, the father says, would be so happy if she'd come. It would mean so much to her. She looks up to Erin. She thinks Erin is *cool*. If Erin would just come to church, it would make her year. And she'll come to Jesus. Erin will. He's sure. She's pretty, is what he doesn't say. If she smiled more, combed her hair back, took the piercings out of her ear cartilage, she'd be marriage material for some nice, scrubbed real estate agent from the congregation.

Erin equivocates. She's booked for a yoga class this Sunday. The father frowns like he suspects yoga of making her heathen. More heathen. His daughter comes to school on Monday with a freshly knotted friendship bracelet just for Erin. Beads reading *WWJD* are tied into it.

Really, she's a sweet kid. She has the earnest, slightly bedraggled look of a kid who had to fight not to be homeschooled. She wants contact with the outside world. Not with other kids, necessarily: her terror's palpable at recess, when she lurks behind storage trailers like the other little monsters might rip out her soul instead of just patches of her hair. But she likes adults. She draws flattering pictures of Erin, and makes a lot of craft projects, and her bean plant in a cup is definitely the best bean plant in a cup. She measures it so *earnestly*.

Erin isn't sure that, if she doesn't come to church, this poor little girl won't be pulled out of school and have to spend the rest of her childhood studying Christian curricula that lie to her about basic details like the age of the world and whether or not Jesus would ride a dinosaur.

So Erin goes along. Puts on a long-sleeved blouse and plain, non-jean pants and lets herself be picked up in front of the school building (*not* at home) at 9:05 on a Sunday morning. She rides in the middle seat of the minivan, with her little girl person. The whole car smells like artificial-cheese-based snacks and apple juice. The parents' attempts at conversation come to her muffled, like voices from some alternate dimension.

From *How are you this morning?* it's a short step to *Why don't you have kids of your own?* and *When will you start a family?* and *I know a nice man you should meet.* And then, at some point, they'll see the inside of her apartment and understand what she really is. It doesn't smell so bad, really. It's home. It's like being ugly on the inside; you keep smiling and no one will ever know.

€ € €

They fucking love her at church. Maybe they love everybody, but Erin suspects she looks too much like fresh meat. Just hip enough to be appealing to the young people. Polite, or at least quiet. Reputed to be good with children.

Is she a Christian? She'd make a lovely Sunday school teacher.

It's a split-second decision.

Yes, Erin says, yes she is. She accepted Jesus as her personal saviour almost ten years ago, and while she hasn't been part of a regular congregation for a while, that's only because she hadn't found the *right* one. She thinks this might be it. Their sense of *fellowship* is so strong.

She's ready to bear witness.

The little girl hits her in the thighs like a charging puppy. Wraps both arms around her legs and weeps.

Erin leans down and hugs her. Hefts, then picks her up. Kid legs wrap around her waist, and there are tears in her hair. Erin says, "Hey, how about you go show me where the Sunday school rooms are, okay?"

❦ ❦ ❦

Erin has been to church exactly three times in her life before this. She just likes watching pirated files of *Big Love* and reading online articles about particularly freaky fundamentalists. She liked *Jesus Camp*. And *Hell House*. Now it's learning material. She reads more. Picks up the language of witnessing and impressing messages on her heart.

Her television habit carries over. The clean, perfect house of television is where these people fucking *live*. Their houses look like that when they invite her over for Bible study. She's deeply worried about it, until she figures out that these people all have housewives. Women who take pregnancy and child care and homemaking very, very seriously. And lots of them *do* homeschool, so she wasn't wrong about that being a serious threat. The homeschooled kids look light-starved, like they're not allowed out of the house by themselves. Erin finds her fingers seized as soon as she's through the door. Little people drag her away to show her their rooms, and she winds up being gone so long the Biblical students settle in without her. She stays upstairs with the kids all evening.

She's so tempted to bring along lessons on particle physics and the origins of the universe. The scientific organization of the universe. At least the poster of the sun rising over the Earth from orbit and Yuri Gagarin saying, *I don't see any God up here.*

It'd be hard to explain to the parents, though, so instead she brings high-powered binoculars. It's a trick she learned from freegans living in a squat in Toronto, that you don't actually need a telescope to take a look at the solar system. A decent pair of binoculars is stronger than Galileo's telescope, so now she's showing kids who've been told God lives on top of clouds how to track the moons of Jupiter. They're long blurs, but she's seen little fingers tracing long, elliptical paths on foggy windows, and that has to be a sign of something. The older ones, who are ten and twelve and fourteen, she talks to them about the anarchist tendencies of the Sermon on the Mount. She smuggles them books by Vonnegut. Missionary from the secular world.

She can't do this in church. But the Sunday school lessons Erin gives ask questions about what happened to Noah's daughters, and in the late winter they make stained-glass art out of tissue paper and she helps her kids inscribe passages from the Song of Solomon around the edges. We are *all* the roses of Sharon and the lilies of the valley. Little girls skipping down the linoleum hallway sing the King James Version in a New International building. They make a skipping rhyme out of it in the gym.

As is the lily in the thorns
So is my love amongst the daughters!
Lily lily lily lily
Turn around the corner! Jump in!
Behold, thou art fair!
Thou hast doves' eyes within thy locks!
Thy hair is as a flock of goats
That appear from mount Gilead!
How many goats are there? Count!

One of the boys shyly brings her a stuffed sheep in the middle of Lent. She's not sure whether it's a pre-Easter gift or a vague proposition that he won't fully understand for another ten years.

❧ ❧ ❧

If she'd given nail polish to the girls, everyone would have traced the mess back to her, but Erin doesn't bother. The girls have soft-pink nail polishes, or clear-coats to keep them from biting their nails.

Erin usually means to paint her nails during lunch hour, so she throws bottles of glittering OPI polish into her purse and forgets them there. Three Lise Watier eye pencils break in the tangled mess before she finally pours it out in the Sunday schoolroom to figure out what left waterproof smears all over her wallet. Bottles tumble onto the floor, mostly (miraculously, because Jesus loves those who enjoy looking like painted whores from time to time) not breaking. Kids scramble to help her pick them up.

Little boy — little? Not really little. Maybe he's eleven. Anyway, she finds him afterwards cradling bottles of Bling Dynasty (gold) and Leaf Him (green), and hiding in the church kitchen.

They're awesome colours. He has good taste. Except, he's scrubbing himself so hard. He tried the colours on, painted individual nails, and it dried fast and hard. She can recognize Thanks So Muchness! (glitter-slut red) and Lucerne-tainly Look Marvellous (grey-green, mysteriously named) on his left hand. He didn't realize, maybe, that it wouldn't wash off. She has to take both his hands to make him stop tearing at his fingers. He's shaking. He's so scared. Though not scared enough not to stuff the bottles in his pockets for later.

She has this moment where she's not sure it's worth fifty dollars in nail polish to help one baby-queer kid play out his fantasies. Not that she remembers to actually *do* her nails, most of the time. And she has tattoos to fall back on. So she shows him those, rolling her sleeves back so he can touch the cherry tree and the climbing dragon and the pin-up girl on her right bicep.

She says, "Don't tell anybody, okay?" And she gives him a mini bottle of nail polish remover. Takes back Bling Dynasty because it's her favourite and gives him a hug.

She has to stop doing this. She should go home and watch TV and maybe convince the English ladies to come help her clean up. Her sink smells unholy. Maybe she should move. It would make her harder to find when the church comes looking.

What turns her in, though, is the Buddha on her thigh. She takes the kids swimming at the Travelodge indoor waterslides, and suddenly her tats are visible to all and sundry, and kids are such fucking tattletales. They don't really have anybody except their parents to talk to. At least public school kids can pass rumours amongst themselves.

Even then, the pastor's only concerned about the example she's setting for the children. He understands that we all struggle, but if she's going to work with the children, she'll need to bring a full testimony. Explain the moment at which she decided to step back from the ways of the flesh, articulate how she came to understand the importance of the purity of her vessel. After that, she can work with the teenagers. She'd make a good youth pastor.

They want her tiny minions back. The kids ratted on her, but really, what else were they going to do? She let them trace the tribal patterns on her back with their fingers.

She can't bring herself to give the parents hell. They're nice people, most of them. Or, at least, they're not actively dangerous. She just doesn't come in, the next Sunday. Sets her junk mail filter to include church bulletins. She screens her calls and shuts down her voicemail. They really do try to get in touch.

At parent-teacher night, she slips around Marcus and Helen, and helps set up science posters that are maybe just a bit too specific about the existence of evolution. They might even assert the legitimacy of the theory. And she puts in for a transfer to the scariest high school in the district. Give her gangling anarchists, please.

She wasn't expecting the kids to take action. Her nail-polish boy needs all the self-protection he can muster. The kid with the binoculars barely talks anyway. They're all "that kid." This is why she needs to teach high school: she can't remember the tiny people's names. All she can see is the tops of their heads anyway.

That kid, the one with the *WWJD* bracelet, she's the one who names Erin as her emergency contact at the hospital. Most of the kids are in hysterics. They can't all be in on the conspiracy. They're God-fearing, Jesus-loving, commandment-reciting Sunday school children. Probably only two or three decided to pour nail polish remover into the communion wine. Erin hadn't even realized that the church did communion. It seems too Catholic for them. And in fact they only do celebrate communion during Lent. The kids must have had to use bottles and bottles of it. Maybe some food colouring to keep the wine from losing its colour.

Erin stands in the waiting room of Emergency, holding one crying kid and patting another, while the infant doctor explains that the parents are going to be fine in a few days. They need emergency contacts to take the kids for the time being, or else they'll have to go with Child Protection.

She can fit seven small kids into her Honda. They share seat belts.

She doesn't ask which one of them did it.

They don't say anything about the state of her apartment. Not even about the smell. Two boys carefully clean off places to sit in her living room. And she does have real food in the fridge. She makes them peanut butter crackers.

When she comes back, the kids have started cleaning. Like they really believe they're going to find the floor. They don't scold her. They do look at her, though, like they're really, deeply *disappointed* that she couldn't tell them about this. Then they file it next to the tattoos and go back to wiping the grunge with vinegar and soft rags. They sing while they work.

If You Lived Here You'd Be Home By Now

PENNY'S CONDO IS GOING TO BE FEATURED ON Home Calls. She's not sure how to feel about that. Not that she doesn't, in spite of herself, wildly want the validation of the hipster-cool online arbiter of interior decorating, but because it's an end point. What do you do with your apartment *after* it's been featured on the Home Calls site? Accept that your home is now complete and you have to stop working on it? Tear the whole thing to pieces and start again? She suspects that only arson might be enough for her to purge the territory her apartment has taken up in her head.

"It's like a painting," says Vinnie, over Japanese tapas. They've paired the food with white wine, because Penny doesn't like sake, and there isn't any point in pretending that she knows enough about Japanese culture to drink it anyway. Her overseas jaunt was to Korea, Japan's nerdy neighbour. But she likes the food, and the feeling that they could be anywhere — Vancouver, Austin, even New York (not Manhattan, of course. Her aspirations aren't *Sex and the City*-based. But maybe Williamsburg or Park Slope). Saskatoon, she tells her friends online, is really coming up.

"What?"

"Your place. It's like a painting. You have to be willing to accept that it's finished, exhibit it, and move on."

Penny sips her wine. "That's not quite right, though. When you finish a painting, it goes away. Somebody buys it, and you start with a new, blank canvas. This is different. It's more like one of those self-help things. At the end of the project, you're stuck with yourself, so you start a new program before you backslide."

Vinnie shakes her head. "Don't get caught up in that. The place isn't *you*. It's just something to do. And you've been doing it a long time. Since I've known you."

"Is it that obvious?" Penny's uncomfortable with the idea. She doesn't want to become one of those women who're obsessed with decorating and won't let anyone walk on the carpet or sit on the furniture. She just likes to arrange her place. She likes finding bits of interesting glass at garage sales, and antique prints of dogs that she can reframe and bunch up on the wall. Weekends she's bored, she takes down all the pictures and rehangs them in different spots, to see what it looks like.

"You show off a bit."

She didn't think she did.

"Not a big deal, honey. Don't feel bad. I'm just saying. I can tell you're proud of it. So show it. And then, while you've got some buzz, sell the place. Buy a new one that's all different inside so it'll need new stuff."

"What'll I do with the stuff I have now?"

"Sell it on eBay."

Penny shakes her head. "I can't." It's hers. Collecting it has marked the last eight years of her life. Since she became an adult. "But I could store it or something."

"Do that. And in a year or two, when you don't care any-more, we'll have the greatest garage sale in the world. You can build it a webpage. We'll develop a fan following, and then have a crowd-funded film project about it." Vinnie grins at her. "Why are we drinking wine? I want a martini."

"Tell the bartender. Are you making fun of me?"

"Only a little bit. You're fun to play with. And I honestly want you to be happy, so exhibit. Let somebody see your work."

Vinnie knows how to pick her words.

Exhibit.

It's not that Penny's disappointed with her life. She has a job she actually sort of likes, and she gets to read interesting books, bum around online, date pretty boys, visit the farmers market on Saturday. She's the queen of brunch. She watched that show on cable where the fierce Polish lady comes along and straight-ens out girls who spend their money on stupid things and run around like they don't care, so now she has a little budget book, and she owns her condo (not outright, but her mortgage is up to date). And Vinnie's right: she could buy a new one. She's vaguely aware that one of the buildings opposite the public library downtown is being refurbished and sold.

This is a lie. She's not *vaguely* aware of anything to do with real estate. The building's been there, part of her small urban world, since she was a kid taking the bus downtown with her dad for Pooh Corner storytime. It has tiny, wrought-iron balconies where people keep bikes instead of barbecues. It's made of brick. On her way home from work, Penny stops by the building. It has a poster in its window listing the website where interested parties can view the new floorplans. There's an email and cell number for a real estate agent. She takes a picture of it with her phone.

At the bus stop opposite the library, she has to wait ten minutes, and while she's reading (off her phone, with one hand above the screen to shade it from the late-afternoon glare), some guy sits down beside her on the bench. She can smell him. It isn't sexy. Penny doesn't want to turn towards him, but she looks. Surreptitiously. Goes ostentatiously back to her phone, because he's *looking* at her. Smiling. One of his front teeth is broken. When the bus comes, she gets up, smiles quickly back — she's not a bitch, and part of *serious urban dwelling* is accepting the proximity of others, even if they aren't the others you'd pick — and joins a woman in a bank-teller suit on a two-person seat. The guy comes close, realizes there's no room with her, or on the other side of the aisle. He moves on back.

€ € €

Penny has a job she actually kind of likes, which isn't something she expected. She has a bachelor's degree in history (honours, thank you), and part of a master's that she abandoned as a bad idea. She worked as a computer transcriber for deaf people for a while. It was easy work, but the keyboarding meant she didn't have to bother to learn sign, and after a year someone explained to her she'd never get a promotion if she couldn't sign, so she had to change. Now she works for the government, in Skills and Retraining.

This makes her, of all things, *a civil servant.* Penny was never interested in politics or political studies. Her area was early twentieth century American history: her thesis was going to be on the social shifts indicated by the wave of etiquette manuals leading up to Emily Post's epic *Etiquette in Society, in Business, in Politics, and at Home.* This, unexpectedly, is why they hired her. Most of the people in Skills and Retraining are social workers, or they come out of either teaching or psychology. They help people figure out what they're going to do, career wise, now that whatever they were doing before is no longer an option. Their offices are full of tissue boxes, and on a given afternoon, the cubicle farm of their office is soundtracked by half a dozen people crying in syncopated off-rhythm.

After they cry it out, the clients are given aptitude tests, some resumé building classes, and a nudge into some non-university course paid for by Employment Insurance. And voila! Baker! Or hotel receptionist, or Class 1A truck driver, or medical office assistant.

This isn't what Penny does, though when she joined the department they gave her the whole short-bus battery of tests. Penny's results said she should be an industrial designer, or else a journalist. She finds those results oddly gratifying, though she doesn't really want to be either one. It's what it says about her: an eye for details, a low-key friendliness, an ear for narrative. She didn't go into the arts, you see, only because she didn't *want* to.

What Penny does is called Professionalization. Her neighbouring cubicle-dwellers call it "Charm School," or "Miss Penny's Finishing School for the Socially Delayed."

She doesn't see every client who comes through the office. Probably not even ten percent of them. She sees the people who repeatedly can't get a job, or can't keep one, and who've been tagged as "lacking presentation." Functionally, this means that they don't come across very well. They have bad table manners. They're not sure how to dress. They show up late or wander off when you stop watching them. They chew their nails during conversations.

They're nerds. Not geeks: Penny calls herself a geek. Geeks

are people who have an obsessional interest in something that the world at large doesn't care about. Geekdom is its own sub-culture of people who decided to own what they love, and do it in spite of the oddity. In contrast, nerds are social disasters. They come across awkward, or fail to grasp that people find them off-putting. It's been one of the small satisfactions of her adult life to discover how often high school cool transforms itself into adult nerdiness. The slightly aggressive disregard for rules that makes you charming at fifteen isn't so appealing at forty. You can smoke up at home, at night, if you want, but showing up stoned is vaguely tragic, bordering on the unemployable.

She begins with basic rules. Most of them have to do with clothing, what you can and can't wear. She learned to tie a necktie for this job, but she came in knowing that the point of the tie should hit the middle of a man's belt buckle. (Television, again, but she owns this. It's her thing, what makes her a geek. She translates pop culture into readable rules for the bewildered. She understands *social capital*. She read Bourdieu. It's what makes her place so spot-on. Her condo is a reflection not just of her, but the social frequency that she's wanted to vibrate at her entire adult life.)

Penny can walk into a room full of donated clothes with you and turn you into a grown-up. While she makes sure your pants fit, and maybe pins a few places for surreptitious sewing, she explains to you where you can get a work wardrobe for cheap.

What they don't always understand is that this sort of thing takes dedication, unless you're rich. Saskatoon isn't, tradition-ally, a town with money. This is part of the problem. For the last couple of generations, being overly done-up was actually a liability. When Penny was a teenager, she noticed that the Pre-mier of Saskatchewan never appeared in-province in a suit. He wore a golf shirt and polyester slacks and drove an old car. She noticed this because he got involved in a national debate on something and showed up on the national news in a gorgeous dark suit, and she didn't register who he was.

The New Saskatoon is a town with some money, and aspirations to not be seen as a redneck dump. You have to make an effort now. Some of the people she sees, it's the first time in their lives they've had to separate "work clothes" from "home clothes." But she's good at this. When she's finished with them, they understand. Their resumés go into a folder so they won't get creased or stained. They clean under their nails. They get jobs, or they don't get jobs, but the feedback that comes into her department doesn't complain about "social deficits." (Maybe there are too many bakers, now. Too many computer-repair people. This isn't Penny's fault. The surplus clients will be re-trained again.)

❦ ❦ ❦

Her submission to Home Calls was put together in a fit of madness after too many raspberry martinis, using a cellphone. She must have taken pictures that were at least in-focus. They emailed her back and asked for better pictures, and a few notes explaining some of the more interesting items on her shelves.

They're going to send a photographer. It'll be someone local, commissioned for the day with a sense of the HC aesthetic. All Penny needs to do — besides make herself up, dress nice, and brush Gibson — is write up her profile.

Penny's design style is *fun and soothing!* Her five essential items are her duvet cover (watercolour-painted silk, done by a friend), her Norfolk Island pine tree, her Eames rocker (she's claiming she found it at a flea market, which is true, once removed — the girl she bought it from on eBay claimed she found it at a flea market), her books, and her collection of tinted-glass telephone insulators. (*I love them! They're found art, with the extra touch of having stories from the people who salvaged them!*) Penny *wants people to be comfortable in her house, and to enjoy being there.*

Gibson raises his head from the bath towel she keeps laid across the foot of the bed to keep the duvet clean, and studies her. He's a massive cat. She rescued him the year she moved home from Korea, and now he's eleven. No well-decorated apartment is complete without a rescue animal. Gibson's real, though. It's all *real*. Most of the place is a part of her, and she loves it. It's pretty and cool in a way she's never quite been able to embody. Differently cool from the burned-out versions of cool who stagger through her office. An edge of *weird*, a whiff of *offbeat*. It's *better* than she is. Still, she can sell it. Start again with different stuff, and go viral in the process. Gibson comes with her.

The cat is an asshole. She likes that about him. She thinks if someone came too close to him on a bus, smelling like the absence of laundry, Gibson might get up and actually shit on them. He's part of her too: the part who smiles so she won't kill everyone and start over.

❦ ❦ ❦

Penny's client Malcolm is a gift from Amy in Counselling. Amy included a sticky note on the file that says, *You might like this one. He's smart. Geeky. That's sort of your thing, no?* Malcolm is not geeky. Or if he is, Penny isn't going to ask him about it. If Amy hadn't insisted in her note that Malcolm was smart, Penny would have presumed he was mildly retarded. He seems confused by her existence, and his shoes are untied.

"How's the search going?" she asks him. She knows how it's going — badly — but it's an easy test to see if he can make small talk.

"Okay."

"Not finding what you want?"

He says, "I guess they aren't. I think the resumé lady didn't explain it very well. She gave me a great score, but I get weird comments when I go interview."

"Oh, yes?"

"Someone gave it — gave my resumé — back to me all marked up like a school assignment. They said they hoped I'd find a good fit soon."

He holds the resumé out to her. It's stapled at one corner, and partially mutilated, but she can't tell whether this is something he's done, or just part of the hiring process' inherent chaos. There's also something slightly off-coloured (brown? grey?) marking the pages. She thinks he's printed it on an old dot-matrix printer; the fanfold edges aren't cleanly torn.

There are, to be clear, spelling and grammar problems on his resumé. This is pretty normal. What she's never seen before is a hiring agent who took the time to point them out. She tells people, *One mistake and it goes in the trash. So proofread!* The line-edits flow like her thesis advisor's notes, so she's on the third page before she realizes that Malcolm has a degree in computer science and one in mathematics. She stares at it. They don't *get* people with degrees. Not that university grads are universally hireable, but Skills and Retraining specializes in people who've been laid off or invalided out of trades. They're short-term solution people.

"You write code?"

"Sometimes. I do algorithms for companies."

"Any demand for that around here?"

"Some. The oil and gas people need stuff done for them."

Penny's still looking at the page. "Tell me what you do for them."

"Really?"

"Sure." She's trying to figure out what the problem is. Looking at the page from one angle and other.

He talks. She realizes that it's more technical than she is and tunes out, nodding and making listening noises. "Nice."

"Yeah?"

She says, "You sound like you enjoy it."

"I really do!"

She looks up. Malcolm is smiling now. He has bad front teeth, and vaguely reminds her of the guy from the bus stop. He has the kind of low-grade stubble she's seen on a lot of tech guys. "Okay, then. I'm glad to hear it. Passion's a real asset. Have you tried telling them what you're telling me, in interviews?"

"I mostly just answered their questions."

"Try talking a bit. Show them you love coding, that it's not just a job for you. That should work. Oh," she hands him back the resumé, "and make the corrections. Whoever did this did you a real favour. If you can clean it up, I think we'll see you placed pretty quick."

"Yeah?"

"You bet."

It's the end of the conversation. She's handed him his stuff, given him some projects. She nods at her cubicle "door." Malcolm leans towards her, just a bit. She resists the urge to lean back.

"Worried about something?"

He says, "I feel like the resumé lady should have caught this stuff."

"Well," Penny tells him, "that's not really her job. She shows you the patterns, but you're supposed to fill in the details." *Because you are an adult and we assume that if you have a degree, then you can read.*

"Is there somebody I can take this stuff to?"

She thinks. "You could check the public library. On the notice board, they put up signs for proofreaders and editors. They'll charge you money, though."

"I maybe won't then. But I'll work on this." He wrinkles his nose. Looks at her.

She wants him to leave. She's starting to understand that Malcolm has some serious social deficits, but he works in tech. He works in *STEM*, the government's baby. He should be hireable even carrying around a dead rabbit.

Science, technology, engineering, and math. It's the litany of the last two provincial administrations. Skills and Retraining even gets pamphlets from the federal government, encouraging them to "encourage and support" clients to move into these areas.

Penny says, "Why don't you work on that resumé. If you're really not confident about it, you can bring it by and I'll have a look at it for you."

"Really?"

She smiles. "Promise."

He's still sitting there. She says, "I'm sorry. I have to see a bunch of people still this morning, but I'll see you soon." Pause. "So you'll have to go, for now."

There. He stands up, gathers his backpack up to his chest and says, "I'm gonna go work on this."

He walks away. Penny stands up, peering over the cubicle top to ensure he's found his way out of the cubicle farm. That he's *really gone.*

❧ ❧ ❧

Malcolm says, "I brought my resumé for you to look at."

He sits in her cubicle. Penny's resisting the urge to lean away. She takes the paper. She doesn't read it, exactly, though she makes a show of marking it with a pen. Malcolm's a problem. She can't figure out what's wrong with him. She feels like he needs a shower or new deodorant, but when she considers it, really, he doesn't smell at all. He *looks like* he smells. He still hasn't shaved, but he doesn't have an interview today. While she's reading, she sees him touch a finger to his tongue. If he reaches for her after that, she can point out to him that saliva carries germs, and hand him her hand sanitizer. He doesn't touch anything. His spit stays on him. It's not an appealing gesture, but it's not really worth addressing.

Instead, she says, "There's a hole in your shirt."

"What?" He looks at himself.

"Up high. By your shoulder." It's not an insignificant hole. The seam's given way near his collar. She makes a note about encouraging him to pay attention to the details of his cloth-ing. He *is* wearing a collared shirt: polo, not button-down, but it's a start. She looks down. His shoes are untied again. They're cheap, black runners, and she thinks a sole might be falling off.

"Have you tried anything from our interview-wear closet?"

"Huh?"

"We keep a bunch of nice-ish office clothes, for interviews. It means you don't have to buy new clothes before you actu-ally get a job."

"I didn't know that."

"We'll go over there in a second." He's fixed the spelling

errors on his resumé, but the grammatical errors are still largely in place. "You didn't finish editing this."

"I did."

"You only did the spelling stuff. You missed the grammar."

"What?"

She shows him the points she's circled, repeating the editorial notations from his last draft: *c/s* for comma splice, *frag* for sentences that aren't complete, *awk* for the selection of "off" passages that she doesn't feel like going into detail over.

"Oh those. I didn't know what those meant."

"You could have asked me."

"I guess."

"Or," and here she looks at him pointedly, "you could have looked them up. You're good enough at tech stuff that I'm pretty sure you know how to Google."

He grins at her. It should be charming: it's a real smile, friendly, like he's decided that she *gets* him. "Yeah."

"Okay, then. Why don't we go hit the closet? And, look. Why don't you sign up for one of the 'Professionalization for Business' seminars? I know you're not in business" — because he's going to say that — "but it's good training for hitting the right note with people who *are* in business."

"I'll think about it."

She's not entirely sure how to fit him from the closet. He doesn't need a suit, just a nice shirt and dress pants. Maybe a tie. But he's that shape she remembers odd guys from high school being — normal-sized legs and shoulders, but bulging in the middle. Nothing sits flat on him. He's not conventionally fat, but she wonders if he's ever had clothes that fit him. Then she wonders why it matters, given what he does for a living. If he made a living.

He doesn't know his measurements in good clothes. Instead,

he tells her "usually XL," and leaves her to estimate and dig and think about how she turned into this chirpy person who sounds *old*. It's because he sounds like a kid. Like he's ten, or fourteen. It's why she thought he was slow: he doesn't look at her like an adult, or carry himself like one. He's huge, but in his head, she's "big." She's his *teacher*, and he doesn't like how she keeps telling him to do his homework.

He says, "How's this?"

He didn't bother with the tie. The shirt's too small in the collar, but he has left far more than just the top button undone. She can see adult acne on his chest, and nipple shadows. So, not a white shirt next time. Blue? Black might hide him a bit. She says, "Not bad, but it's not the seventies."

"What?"

"Button it up a bit." Buttoned up, she's aware of his bulk. His odd legs stick out under his body, which sticks out and strains against the shirt. "Right, different shirt."

A bigger shirt just looks too big on him. The pants need a belt. She tells him so, but that he's welcome to "sign out" the clothes any time he has an interview. She'll give him the item numbers for them. They don't have men's shoes. No one donates them to the government. She tells him to have a look at Value Village for black loafers.

"Loafers?"

"Google it."

"Right!"

Malcolm dips in, suddenly, and hugs her. She resists the urge to smash an elbow into his trachea. He's too close. His hands are appropriately high, at her shoulders, but his chest is close to her face, and it's uncomfortable in a way that makes her want to give up sex for a while. At close range, she and Malcolm are almost exactly the same age. Facially, she wonders, would he show up decently in an online profile? If he didn't show his teeth?

He goes away, finally. Penny lets herself into the records-box room and sits on the floor.

Malcolm has a file on the computer system, but it's privacy-restricted so that she can only see as much information as the system thinks is relevant to her job. In the boxes, though, are Amy's notes, and it turns out, Carol's notes, and Jessamyn's notes. Malcolm is contagious. You can catch him from your co-workers.

Their notes aren't helpful. They all say the same things: "smart" and "social deficit?" Jessamyn thinks he might have Asperger's, with a note that he should be tested, but she didn't refer him to anyone. It might not help. Penny has a list of support systems she can refer people to, but there isn't much for adults on the autism spectrum. Lots for pre-teens, some for teenagers. Nothing for grown-ups. She remembers that Vinnie keeps a laminated copy of a *Calvin & Hobbes* cartoon that says, *In my opinion, we don't devote nearly enough scientific research to finding a cure for jerks.*

Vinnie doesn't show it to just anybody. She'd never take it to work. Vinnie works with "developmentally disabled" adults in a group home, teaching basic life skills. She's good at it. But she has it easy: the clients she works with, people can tell what's wrong with them. Nobody expects them to pass for normal.

Penny mutters to herself, "Until they're eighteen we call them autistic. After that we call them mathematicians."

Farther down in the box is Malcolm's intake form. His financials. His marital status. Malcolm is married. He has three kids. Penny stares. Malcolm has serious financial problems. A spotty work history. Shining credentials.

He's married. He has three kids. She can't even picture it.

❦ ❦ ❦

She knows what's wrong with Malcolm. He's gross.

Penny looks at Vinnie, who's helping her choose clothes for her photo shoot. "Don't judge me."

"I am judging you, just a bit."

"You don't remember when you were a kid, there was that gross kid?"

There was always the gross kid. He wore sweatpants all the time. His T-shirts were stained. He had a really short haircut, and bad dandruff anyway. He looked like maybe he didn't wear underpants. Kids debated whose job it was to tell him about deodorant.

Penny has a portfolio of gross kids. She was, in gossip, "romantically linked" with every single one she went to high school with. Penny is a nerd and she likes gross boys.

Penny says, "I'm going to call off the photo shoot."

"What?"

"I'm not *finished* yet."

"Penny." Vinnie sits her down. "Did you ever figure out what this shoot is worth?"

"No, but I asked a real estate agent."

"And?"

"He said plus twenty thousand to the selling price, or plus thirty if I sell it mostly furnished."

"Jesus."

"I know." She'd never had anyone put a price tag on her sense of style before.

"So?"

Penny is not a nerd. She has fun sex with pretty boys she finds online. She has a job she mostly likes.

"I could buy the downtown apartment. Did I show it to you?"

"So pretty. Red cabinets?"

"Blue-based red. Not fire-engine. It looks like sex in kitchen form."

"Try on this dress. See if you think you'll clash with the couch."

€ € €

Malcolm has three unsuccessful interviews. He officially looks good on paper. Penny sends him to Professionalization Group, in the hopes that somebody else will tell Malcolm that he's gross and needs to get it together. Malcolm comes to every day of Professionalization Group. He takes notes in a binder. He groans like a kid when she emphasizes table manners and "clean" presentation — *that means your spit stays in your mouth and your hands stay in your lap. If you're itchy, invest in Gold Bond. People want you to look catalogue-shiny. You only have to fake it long enough to get hired. Remember, you have to be* better *than you are, for that one hour. I mean. Not "better." They'd call it "better." You need to be shiny. Learn to fake it. Chin up. Smile. Show up ten minutes early. Bring a clean copy of your resumé. Don't break their hand when you shake hands. Make sure your nails are clean.*

The group runs practice interviews. Malcolm talks about his love for mathematical problem solving. The woman opposite him leans back. Penny watches her reach for hand sanitizer as Malcolm walks away. Penny gives everybody feedback. Positive stuff orally, so they can hear themselves praised in front of others. Constructive "better next time" notes on paper. She makes eye contact with people. Smiles at them. Malcolm shifts under her gaze.

Over lunch, at her desk, Penny logs on to Adult Finder and posts a come-on, then deletes it. Goes into FireLife and posts under *Intimate Encounters* instead.

She runs the afternoon sessions, on grooming and clothing. When she gets back to her desk, there's a note from IT, not addressed to her personally, noting that *non-professional sites have been blocked to avoid abuse of resources.* Penny checks her profile on her phone. Two out of three responses are badly spelled. The third is a dick pic. She sends a note back to the more literate of the first two. Agrees to meet him for coffee at a Starbucks on Eighth. On her way, she calls Vinnie and says, "Text me at 6:15."

"Are you on a date?"

"I'm going to go get laid."

Vinnie texts her at 6:15. Penny texts back *im okay*. Later, she texts Vinnie the guy's name, phone number, and address, because Penny's going home with him, and someone should know where she is in case he kills her.

She does this. It's one of the rules of the Internet that an ordinary-looking girl can get laid when she wants to, as long as her standards aren't too high. She meets a lot of guys who might be clients of hers but aren't. They have apartments on one edge of the city or the other, with cheap furniture and fleece blankets covering both the couch and the bed. They're not quite as good in bed as they think they are, but she has fun, enough fun to make it usually worth her time. She takes a shower in his slightly dusty bathroom, ignoring the boxers clumped behind the door. He gets in with her and plays with her breasts. Afterwards, he puts on Axe-style body spray. It smells awful, but also like male bodies, and she forgets herself and licks his shoulder blade. Rinses out her mouth twice to get rid of the rubbing-alcohol taste.

He drives her back to the Starbucks after, and buys her a chocolate almond biscotti, "Just 'cause."

"Thanks."

"Look, this is my cell number. The one I gave you before is my work number. Call me sometime, if you want to hang out," he says.

Penny takes the bus home and thinks about what kind of guy would give out his work number instead of his cell. Somebody unembarrassed to have strange women call him on the job, but who doesn't want to talk to girls at two in the morning if they're pregnant or infected.

He smelled really good. His body spray and low-grade sweat are still on her skin, so she rolls on her bedspread to preserve the smell.

⋹ ⋹ ⋹

Malcolm comes by her office at least twice a week. Penny tells him that because her schedule's crowded these days, he needs to make appointments through the front desk. He does. He shows up for every single one.

He's frustrated. She wants to be sympathetic. Professionally, she is. It sucks that a guy with his credentials can't get a job in a boomtown. He can't read people. She doesn't think he's autistic. He's high-verbal. Once he decided Penny was okay, he started talking like an explosion. He talks through what he thinks his problems might be. He tells her he's worried about the future.

She says, "Is your wife working?"

"Part time."

She isn't supposed to know he's married. He has three kids. He didn't tell her, but she's realized that most of their clients think the government has an exhaustive file on everybody. They get annoyed if she *doesn't* know everything. She had a woman once who asked Penny to just look up her medical records so that she could get a prescription refill while she was in.

"You guys okay?" Penny asks.

"It's expensive. School supplies and school fees both come up this month."

She thinks, *times three.*

Penny can't imagine who would marry the gross kid. She wants to not picture him having sex.

She can't fix him.

He keeps *hugging* her. It's not sleazy. He keeps his hands to himself. She'd complain about harassment, but she didn't complain the first six times, and now it's an established pattern. She keeps telling him to be warm and friendly with people. Negative feedback might break him, and then he'll be in her office forever.

She calls down to IT to see if they need anybody. They don't, and she thinks the guy on the phone has been reading her Intimate Encounters listing. Not for sex, just to judge her. Morally.

She thinks about leaving some of her passwords visible, or emailing one down there by mistake. Her profile's as much a work of art as her apartment. Both are curated versions of the most appealing parts of her. Slightly arty, desirable in a way that's not quite quantifiable. It's worth twenty to thirty thousand dollars in the current market. *Be impressed, asshole.*

The new apartment is a thing of beauty. As the renovations progress, they've been posting photos online for prospective buyers. Where the floors could be salvaged, the original hardwoods have been preserved. Areas with extensive damage or poor quality linoleum have been upgraded to dark-finish bamboo. There's a rumour, just a rumour, of gas ranges being added.

It's not the apartment of a civil servant. Her current condo is civil-servant grade: it's off-white and beige, and has cheap cabinets that she repainted pistachio green one by one. The new place isn't blandly middle class, though, either. It's the apartment of an artist, or a hipster in the best sense of the word. It's cool. Geeky-cool. It's going to be more part of her than her current place has ever been. She'll give up every telephone insulator to get it.

≪ ≪ ≪

He stands at a normal distance, and it's too close to her. Whenever Malcolm visits, Penny feels like deleting the Axe-smelling boy's cell number from her phone.

She didn't know this could happen to an adult. What's wrong with Malcolm is something she thought people grew out of. An awkward phase lasting your whole life is too much of a nightmare. You're supposed to go to university, find your tribe, shed your nerd-skin and put on a geeky one that's a combination of coolness and obsessive competence. You work crap jobs for a couple of years, develop a career, build yourself a life, find someone to marry, and have kids or else travel. Go to Thailand. Collect art.

Penny says, "Amy?"

"Yeah."

"Why'd you send me Malcolm?"

Amy looks up from her keyboard. She says, "Yeah, sorry about that. Malcolm's..."

"I don't know what's wrong with him."

"He isn't stupid."

"I know."

"Do what you can for him, okay?"

He's married. He has three kids. His wife works part time.

Did she drop out of university because she got pregnant? Is she like him? They'd have been surprised, both of them, to discover someone desired them. They wouldn't have internalized safe-sex lessons, because they didn't think it would ever come up. Or they were unlucky and awkward, the way they've always been, and the condom failed, and they wouldn't have been able to decide what to do until it was too late for an abortion. So they got married. And she dropped out and he stayed in school. They must have a nauseating amount of student debt.

Penny thinks they probably live on the west side of the city. She didn't look that up. But they'd fit there, at least a bit, and it's cheaper. There are three-bedroom apartments that, until the boom, you could get for under a thousand dollars a month, and if they're on a decent lease, it might still be cheap enough to live there, with two kids in one room, and one in the other. No, she thinks. The kids each have their own room. Malcolm and his wife sleep in the living room, on the hide-a-bed. They keep their clothes on a rolling garment rack that the kids knock over when they're playing. Everything is for the kids. Malcolm tries to keep his computer away from them, and he and his wife fight about that, but everything's for the kids, so he maybe gives up the computer, too.

Penny doesn't know what to do with him. She doesn't have the power to refer people. Malcolm's been through their entire office. To get him off her client list, he either has to be hired, leave on his own in frustration, or be removed by security.

She thinks about it while she's making dinner. The kitchen looks good — clean piles of antique dishes perch in the cupboards, bamboo boxes hold up her utensils. She's slicing a chicken breast to fry — half the pieces will go in her Mexican ranch chicken salad tonight. The rest will go in a sandwich for tomorrow, with pesto and tomato. On ciabatta bread! She used to buy the sandwich at Safeway, but her budget didn't include buying lunch every day, so she's learned to cook most of her favourites.

Bits of fat and cartilage come away under her knife. She has no idea why that small, rectangular cartilage-end shows up in every single boneless chicken breast. Her office refers a dozen people a year to become meat-cutters. They can't all be incompetent. She doesn't know, though. The meat-cutters never seem to need professionalization. She has a theory they've been carving up their job-market competition and selling the pieces to chain barbecue restaurants. If there are few enough of them, no one will complain about their little quirks.

The fat bits in her palm are so soft. They'd liquify if she cooked them. Penny thinks about it. For a second, it looks like release. She can rub the liquified fat on a piece of paper, leave it in her guest chair before Malcolm comes in. It'll soak into the upholstery and into his pants. (His pants are a loss anyway. She's gotten used to the looseness of the track pants and the way it suggests a gross-kid state of no underwear, but lately they're stained, too. He'd be better off with anything from Value Village.) When he's gone — half an hour after the longest she can really stand talking to him — she'll call their security guard and point out the mess. Suggest it's . . . well. She should tell the guy it's come. Semen. That she won't pursue it legally, but she doesn't want them to admit Malcolm to the office ever again. For real authenticity, she should add just a little tapioca.

She isn't going to do it, but she needs a mental break. Just a little one. So she cooks the mess up together — chicken fat and minute-tapioca — and pours the whole lot into a sour cream container. Sticks it in the fridge for heating up later in the microwave. Then goes back, gets a Sharpie, and puts an X on the lid, so she won't eat it by accident.

⤆ ⤆ ⤆

Penny and Gibson's Fun and Soothing Urban Retreat is the Friday House Tour!

Penny wears a vintage-styled polka-dot sundress. Gibson curls deeply into the bit of sheepskin she's laid in the Eames rocker for him. Any decent person would want this life. This home, this cat, this crooked smile.

She lists the condo with the assessing real estate agent three days before the post goes up. He sets up a little link so that prospective buyers can go from the Multiple Listing Entry to the Home Calls feature.

The actual offer comes in at eighteen thousand above market. Penny's disappointed. It's more than she paid, and it'll cover the unexpected price jump on the downtown apartment, but she has had to scale down exactly how sexy-expensive that version of herself is. She's sad. Existentially. It's like looking in the mirror at the wrong angle, and thinking, *I hate my cheekbones.*

She's going to call the Starbucks boy so she can smell his short, bristly hair, but instead she catches the bus that stops just half a block from her (now/soon former) building. Rides it downtown, takes the transfer, and continues out to West-gate. On west-side busses, the company is different. Fewer people wear earbuds, and no one plays with their phone, so she has to leave hers in her pocket. She gets off at the defunct Bowlarama. The low-rise apartment blocks are dense, here. Inside the enclave, behind the noise-reduction walls, there's only a Mac's full of teenagers buying slush drinks.

There are no sidewalks. For a while, she walks on the angled curb, using a sense of balance that she honed in gymnastics when she was six. Sharp as a six-year-old, she stumbles off the curb and into the street and nearly falls in front of a car. She walks on the grass, after that. Leaves her shoes on because the lawns are thick with shattered dark brown bottles. One slip and she's going to need a tetanus shot.

She's looking for Malcolm. She never did look up his address, and there's a chance he actually lives in the other enclave, north of here, but she has a bet with herself. And it's quiet. There are *vacancy* signs hanging from the wooden plaques naming each complex. *The Regent's Arms. Tamarack Place. Silver Gardens. Centennial Park* has a small plastic sign thrust into its glassy lawn: *If you lived here, you'd be home by now.* It's as good a sign as any. She turns into the parking lot and walks around to find the common area in back.

There's a small playground. Adults are sitting on the picnic benches smoking while their kids shriek. In the half-dark, there are people trying to read: mostly fantasy novels and magazines, but she sees a few illuminated screens. People are texting. A woman with a blonde ponytail steps under the hand-over-hand bars to rescue a little girl who's stranded. Penny can hear her grunt. Having kids seems to induce bad backs: if they don't tear your muscles during delivery, the kids climb you until you break. The woman limps, hauls the little one over to a bench and drops her into the glow of a laptop screen.

Penny's good. She called this just right: the man with the laptop is Malcolm. He doesn't look up from the screen, just pulls the little girl into his lap and presses his face into her hair for a second. Penny thinks the girl must be about four. Two more kids out in the half-dark are his.

If she steps up just a bit, he'll be able to see her. His wife could see Penny already, if she turned this way. It smells like August and vaguely like the storm water retention pond where ducks are swimming. Penny steps back, instead, and leans against the rough-cut painted planks of the building wall. A woman standing there already hands her a lit cigarette. Penny holds it for a while. It goes out, and the woman takes it back, hisses at her, walks away in disgust.

Penny sits down with her back against the building, and watches people collect their kids. It's getting dark. Even Malcolm closes his laptop and tucks it under one arm, the little girl under the other. He never turns toward Penny. No one challenges her presence. As far as any of them are concerned, she just lives here.

Invisible City

JAY GOT OFF THE BUS IN GOOSE LAKE WITH HIS backpack and August riding in the carrier on his chest. Goose Lake wasn't much of a town, but at least he could walk here without people staring. Just a guy with a baby. She didn't smell so good. He walked with her to the gas station by the highway and asked for the restroom key.

They were selling bannock at the counter, with little restaurant-packets of strawberry jam. The guy holding the key looked at him. "You Buttercup's ex?"

Wrong word. It wasn't like they'd broken up. Jay said, "Yeah."

"I'll call Rachel while you're in the can. She'll come get you."

Jay had eight dollars, which was enough for either diapers or a few basic food things, and he was going to have to decide which to buy before the grandmother turned up and had a look at him.

She might have food, but she wasn't going to have diapers. He bought one of the little generic packs they had in the back aisle. The guy rang him up. "Band number?"

Behind him, someone rattled one off.

It was how he met Rachel McLeod.

He'd forgotten Rachel was August's *great*-grandmother. She wasn't ancient, though. She was just an old lady in jeans and a *Goose Lake Chuckwagon Championships 1991* T-shirt and a ratty fleece vest.

Jay said, "I don't have a band number."

"August does. Come on. I'll make you dinner." She paused at the door. "Give me the baby."

He thought about doing it. He'd handed August to at least half a dozen people in her tiny life, and only four of them were nurses. Only one of them was Buttercup. He meant to let Rachel look at her grand-baby, but his arms both wrapped around the carrier and he didn't lift her out.

He rode like that, holding August against his chest in the passenger seat of Rachel's dirt-blue Lumina, down the sand roads to the ferry. Over the river and into the hills, and they were on Indian land before he remembered that babies were supposed to ride in carseats, and never in the front seat, though he couldn't exactly remember why not. Rachel glanced at him.

"It doesn't have airbags. You're safe."

Jay didn't like Rachel, but his bones did what she told him. He got out in her yard and let the dogs sniff his legs, and followed her into the house. He sat down when she told him to. Eventually, August squirmed until he had to put her down, and then he couldn't catch her before she made a crawling run at the dogs sleeping by the washing machine.

"They won't eat her. They've got some experience. Eleven grandkids, six great-grandkids, no dog fatalities. I told Mike to leave his sled team up north. There isn't anything in the house or the yard that'll eat her."

She gave Jay a bowl of soup and a sleeve of salted-top crackers, and she ate with him. Drank tea and gave him some when he asked. Jay chewed. Thought about the joke Buttercup had told him about the Indian who drank tea all day and that night he drowned in his tea pee.

Rachel waited until he was finished, and then she gave him a handful of store-bought oatmeal cookies and said, "So explain to me how you're the girl who got Buttercup pregnant."

€ € €

Buttercup was always about halfway to being a pretty girl. She bleached her hair and it wound up like straw, a shade lighter than her skin. When she got out of the shower and her hair was dark from being wet, she looked the most like the way Jay pictured her when she wasn't around. The least breakable. She wore jeans and a T-shirt with glittery flowers on it the day he met her.

They went to a party. It was on Robinson Street, up past the rail yards, and it was maybe the best party he ever went to.

He knew a few of the guys who hosted it from work. Brent test-played every guitar that came into the shop, and he had a couple of them at home. He knew guys who were in the folk scene and guys who did hip-hop. They brought hand drums, jammed together in the living room until it was so loud Jay had to retreat to the back yard. They'd built a fire in the pit, and people were tucked up close around it to keep the mosquitoes off. Somebody gave him a beer. Buttercup had a six-pack of rum coolers, sticky with artificial strawberry. She said she'd never got a taste for anything straight. Someday she wanted a kitchen where she could make her own margaritas and daiquiris.

The difference, she explained, was tequila vs. rum. A good daiquiri needed white rum, and fresh fruit crushed up with ice. She'd had one made by a girl who lived near where she grew up. They'd mixed it up and hung out on the lawn-swing all afternoon.

Which, Jay gathered, was Buttercup's way of saying she had maybe a thing for girls. He had to tell her he wasn't one.

"I know. You're sort of . . . mixed. Not just one thing. Brent told me so I wouldn't freak out. He said I should make you go have some fun."

Jay did have fun. He danced with Buttercup when she asked, and then he went down to the basement with her.

They'd built a city down there. Out of Lego. For real.

Buttercup had been in on that project for a long time. There were ten or so people working on it. Every time they found cheap Lego at a garage sale or off-brand cheap at the Giant Tiger, they brought it in. There were other toys incorporated, too — blocks and some of the massive baby-sized Lego he saw around, and other things like the plastic string that you could weave into friendship bracelets.

"Is it supposed to be Winnipeg?"

She shook her head. "It's the Invisible City."

The Invisible City, she explained, was sort of everywhere built-up, everywhere that wasn't country, but it also wasn't most places. One of the original residents of the house — he hadn't lived there for a couple of years — had liked this book by an Italian writer. Buttercup tried it and got lost towards the middle, but the idea of the Invisible City stuck.

The basement held a scale model of what was almost present. There were complicated, interconnected buildings between the low-rise ones. Some of them reached to the insulation-wrapped hot-water pipes, almost six feet up.

She offered him the chance to build something. A new space had opened up when water damaged the cardboard boxes in the corner and everything in them had had to be thrown away.

He built for hours. Most of the city he imagined was low, like the stretches of Kildonan he'd bounced around before he was a teenager. The house he made, though, started narrow at the bottom and then got complicated. It grew outwards mostly on one side. He had to use string to rig it up. Stapled the free ends to the wall-board to hold the whole thing suspended at the edge of the remaining open space.

"That has to be symbolic."

"I never have enough room."

"Do you want me to leave?"

He said, "What?"

"Am I too close?"

"What? No. I wasn't counting you."

"Good."

Later, when they were curled together on an air mattress upstairs, she took his clothes off. He hadn't had surgery yet, then, but he strapped his tits down as hard as he could. They were little, from the shots, and his hips had changed. She straddled him and looked. Nodded.

You fuck guys for money, she told him later, *and what you want when you get home is something completely different.*

€ € €

He wondered if Rachel could challenge him. Drag him to court and take August away. She could probably prove . . . something. Jay'd been in court twice; he had dreams about being there again and not being able to make anybody hear him.

What Rachel actually said was that if he wanted to go off on his own, she'd take care of August for him. Like it would be some kind of favour.

Rachel didn't have the warm old-lady friendliness he asso-

ciated with the word "grandma." She was simultaneously older
than dirt and fast on her feet, so that when she picked August
out of Jay's arms, she didn't even grunt.

He thought about witches who stole babies in stories.

She said, "You're going to need somewhere to live."

He wouldn't have agreed to live with her, but she didn't
offer. Buttercup had told him she grew up in a house with
twelve people in it — two sisters, her mom, her mom's
boyfriend, her uncles, five cousins. It was one of the reasons
she'd loved their tiny place in Winnipeg, which only had three
people in it. She could go into the bathroom and lock the door,
and stay in there for half an hour before Jay started asking
when she might be out.

The cabin Rachel had on offer was in back of her place, and
it wasn't exactly a house.

Jay'd had a friend for a while who was cousins with a rich
family, and she'd invited Jay to come up to the "cabin." It wasn't
anything Jay would have called a cabin. It was bigger than his
foster mom's place: two storeys, and a big deck, plus a balcony,
and it was made of this bright, raw wood that must have taken
a lot of work to turn into a single, glossy surface. There was
satellite TV.

Rachel's cabin was more what he'd been picturing. It had
a couple of rooms, and windows, and a wood floor. Its siding
had been put on a long time ago, but decades after the cabin
was built. Underneath, where it was hanging off, he could see
grey bark on the original boards.

The outhouse was nearby, but pointedly outdoors. So was
the little pump.

Rachel pointed at the pump. She said, "It's safer than having
the open well, when that one starts walking. The water's okay
to drink. They tested it a while ago. And it's capped, so nothing
can fall in."

The cabin had electricity. There was a wire run over from Rachel's house, leading to a light hanging from the ceiling of the kitchen, and there was an old fridge. The stove was ancient, iron, and wood-powered.

He was going to have to learn to chop wood.

Somewhere for him to live. Rachel gave him some food and some baby crackers, and a sleeping bag to put on the old mattress. Some garbage bags he could lay over the mattress if the smell of it got to him, or he was worried about August making it worse.

Left him there.

He wasn't prepared for the quiet. Rachel's house was only fifteen yards away, but he couldn't see it through the trees. The grass was deep against his knees. Insects all around him, enough that he instinctively shielded August's face.

Eventually, August squirmed in his arms and he put her down in the grass. She bit at it with her mostly-toothless mouth. Laughed.

Like a fairy tale, except that it locked him into this burning quiet instead of a tower. Witch at the gate.

❧ ❧ ❧

He walked back to Rachel's house after dark, because he couldn't sleep. She was sitting up, at the kitchen table. She wasn't alone.

Her house was full of kids, some of them only a bit bigger than August, but most of them nine or ten. She'd left cookies on the table for them. They were piled up on the couch, watching a movie on the CBC.

Jay said, "Good picture."

"They gave us a satellite. Just for the channels we got over the air until they fucked up the digital shift, and we were left with no TV at all for a year. Kids went nuts." Rachel was smoking.

Jay jerked his hand toward the cigarette, to put it out, to remind her that August was *right here*. Rachel twisted away. "When they aren't all here, I watch that learning channel out of Lloydminster. They have shows about English farms and stuff. It's pretty good. Why are you here?"

I'm lonely. It's too quiet. "Couldn't sleep."

"Nobody can sleep. It's party night. Have you been listening?"

He shook his head.

"It's why they're all here. Their folks are off partying. Maybe not safe for the kids. So they're here. They'll pass out in a couple of hours. You can come back for breakfast, if you want." She considered. "There's some books in a box in the porch, if you're bored."

He was bored. The books were shit, but he took three. Rachel liked romance novels, he guessed. They were library discards, mostly. Some of them were newish: Christian romances, stories about Amish girls, invocations to prayer. The box was supervised by an annoyed-looking Jesus.

When he laid down on the bed to read, he discovered there was another Jesus in the rafters, looking down on him.

❧ ❧ ❧

He didn't go to that party, or the next party. He stabilized the wiring in the cabin, and then traced it back to Rachel's house and fixed her breaker box so it wouldn't blow or catch fire. She gave him some venison stew and a bag of secondhand baby clothes for August.

He didn't go to the parties. He fixed stuff, and let August play outside, and tried not to think about Buttercup. He'd tried again, before he left Winnipeg, to report her missing. Left his name with the police, and a "care of" for the Almighty Voice First Nation. Gave them Rachel's name, too. In case.

The party found him, though, like a team looking for one more guy so they wouldn't have to forfeit. They came into Rachel's yard and barrelled right past her. Found Jay trying to fix a remote-controlled car one of the kids had abandoned in the grass.

"You Buttercup's ex?"

"I'm Buttercup's husband."

Just a minute while the guy looked at him. Raised his chin a bit.

"Okay. Anyway. What's your name?"

"Jay Dudley."

"Tansi. So we're having a thing tonight. Thought you might wanna come."

"An actual party," Jay asked, "or just getting drunk?"

Almost an actual party. There was music, but only because Jay hooked up the speakers and fixed the wiring. It made him popular. A girl slid up behind him and kissed his neck, gave him a handful of CDs. She whispered, "You're the DJ now." It must have been true, because everybody ran out to their trucks and shitty cars and brought back their entire CD collections. Most of it was stuff you could buy in gas stations, or that other people were selling off, country and 80s rock. The unlabelled discs were more interesting. They were home recordings, people's hip-hop and rock bands. Stuff people had traded for or found or burned off the Internet.

He balanced it as best he could. Switched out the discs whenever he'd had enough of something. Accepted beers and kisses from girls, and all-over body hugs from guys who towered over him.

The girl who'd kissed him first showed him her fancy shawl for pow wows, and the box of ribbons and glass beads she was using to make one for her cousin. Then pushed him back on the bed. Crawled up to straddle him and kissed him hard. "You're fucking cute," she whispered against his neck.

Jay shivered. Didn't pull himself together until after she'd unbuttoned his shirt. He let her stare. His pectoral scars were livid against his skin; all his blood had fled downward. She prodded one, experimentally.

"What're these?"

Jay said, "That's what was left after they cut my heart out."

He'd been waiting for years to use that line. Buttercup would have called bullshit on him. Fancy-shawl-dancer rocked back against his hips.

"They cut off your dick, too?"

"I'm married," Jay said. "Not interested. Thanks, though."

"Nobody's that not interested."

"Come by my place sometime and I'll tell you all about it." He wrapped his arms around her shoulders and rolled her down. Kissed her and humped hard against her thigh for a minute. "Another time."

He walked out before she could grab him, and proceeded to get very, very drunk. He threw up behind the house and stared up at the sky. Amazing stars. They almost gave enough light to see. He thought he could find the road. The music from the house throbbed hard enough he could use it as a compass point: move away from that, towards the dark and the quiet.

Walked home. Two miles or so along the gravel, watching for car lights and dodging into the ditch as they came shooting by. He stepped in a huge hole and fell. Ripped the knee of his jeans open.

He found a porcupine and tripped over it. Got quills in his shins.

When he showed up on her doorstep, Rachel wouldn't let him in. "You're drunk."

"I want August."

"No baby as long as you're drunk. Go sleep it off."

He laid on his back on the bed with the windows open, listening to the plastic under him squeak. It occurred to him, before he fell asleep, to roll over. If he wanted to drown, he could hike out to a slough and do it that way. If he choked in bed, Buttercup wouldn't forgive him. When he tried to roll over, the quills ground deeper into his legs.

❦ ❦ ❦

He couldn't get the quills out on his own. He tried using pliers, but the spikes wouldn't come free. Rachel found him like that, bloody and still quilled into his jeans. She took him into her house and ran a hot bath. Filled it with vinegar first, and then baking soda, like a massive science experiment that fizzed while she cut his jeans away. Jay flinched away from her. She poked a quill in his shin pointedly.

"I doubt you've got anything I haven't seen before, just maybe a bit rearranged. But if it makes you happy, you can keep your shorts on. Sit."

She left him there in the tub, in a wet T-shirt and shorts, soaking in the stinking mess and whimpering softly at the state of his legs. Goddamn animals. Walking around.

"You don't get to get revenge," Rachel told him. She gave him a cup of coffee. "Porcupines aren't for killing. Unless you're lost. Then you can kill one with a stick and eat it. They're pretty easy to stab."

Jay realized he'd heard that before, from an old guy who claimed to have done it a couple of times. He was from way north, though. "I thought that was a Chippewa rule."

"It's a good rule. Don't go killing the porcupine." She poked the quills again. Grabbed sewing scissors and cut the ends off of each. "It'll take the pressure off. They're getting softer."

She pulled him up from the bath and pulled the softened quills out with Jay's pliers. Looked at the broken bits sadly. "I could've used those, if you weren't such a baby."

"For what?"

"Moccasins for your girl." She gave him a couple of Tylenol and a pink pill that turned out to be Benadryl and put him to sleep for the rest of the day. When he woke up, it was night. Rachel came by when he turned on the lights and told him she'd got him a job in town, so he had to get off his ass in the morning.

❧ ❧ ❧

Someone told somebody else that Jay Dudley could fix electronics, so Brent McGowan took him on at the tiny hardware store where they fixed vacuum cleaners and little old ladies' TV sets and, Jay learned, specialized in repairing the old, cabinet-sized, vacuum-tube TVs.

Jay's hours were restricted to what Jennifer Dustyhorn worked at the grocery store, because she had a car and he didn't. He paid her five bucks a day for gas, which he thought was insane until he saw how much she paid for it. She had three little kids and lived with her mom and her aunt in a house three miles over from Rachel's.

"So you know," Jennifer told him while they were driving, "I don't want a man. My mom keeps trying to set me up with guys, and she thinks maybe if you can keep a job, I'll like you. But I'm not looking. So we're clear." She didn't want to see August, or really know anything about Jay. He didn't bug her. She showed up at ten to eight, and if he wasn't ready, she'd leave without him.

The first day, he left August with Rachel. It made his skin

crawl, not knowing exactly where August was, and he still wasn't sure Rachel wouldn't just take her. She'd come from somewhere up north, and she still had people up there. It wouldn't be too hard for her to go back, with August tucked into the passenger seat of Rachel's ancient car, and just disappear into the bush, then claim she'd never heard of Jay to begin with.

He thought about it while he worked.

Brent McGowan was a white guy, medium-old, who'd been there since Goose Lake was a cowboy town. He'd figured out his market, he said, and so he bought vacuum tubes at flea markets and on the Internet. He knew how to make a few, too, in the basement. "If you stick around, I might show you."

Brent's local-market work, he explained, was a side-business. He made his real money restoring vintage TV sets for collectors. They shipped the TVs to him, usually by bus and sometimes from other countries, big cabinet sets weighing a couple of hundred pounds apiece. Jay'd seen those all his life. He grew up in houses where the main set was one of these huge, furniture-sized creations with a dwarfed, warped screen. Everything he saw on them was blurred and dependent on rabbit ears, except in one house where they'd jerry-rigged it for cable. The picture didn't look any better than the over-air broadcast, but there were more channels.

The TVs had developed a cult following of people who claimed that you couldn't get a real, fundamental television experience on a modern set. They were mostly the same people who'd revived cassette tapes, and who kept Beta video players around, never watching anything that was made more recently than two or three years before Jay was born.

"It's what they like, and they're willing to put money into it. Somebody noticed I was digging around online for parts, so now this is most of what I make my money on."

The high-end restoration jobs Brent did himself, in a private workshop. He'd go off for the whole day "for parts," and come back with sealed, scuffed boxes. He left Jay in charge.

Jay did mostly not much. He messed with people's broken ghetto-blasters until they worked and charged whatever seemed fair, or whatever he thought they could pay. When Brent went off for a week to Calgary, Jay started bringing August to work. He made a playpen out of heavy cardboard boxes, and picked her up a couple of soft toys at the Mennonite secondhand store next to the credit union.

Goose Lake wasn't quite the TV fantasy of a small town Jay'd been fed most of his life, but it was cool to be able to watch most of what happened in an entire town go on outside the dirty glass display window. The one commercial street ran perpendicular to the service road with the gas stations and the grain terminal. Old people wandered around for hours, just getting the air. The old white people went for coffee and pointedly didn't look at him. The old Indian people stopped by to ask him about his family.

They were fucking nosy.

They wanted to know everything about him. They already knew he was living at Rachel's place, and that he was married to one of Rachel's granddaughters. They wanted to know who his parents were. Where he'd grown up. What tribe was he? What nation were his people from? How much proper language did he know? Could he cook? Hunt? Did he drink? Did he come to ceremonies?

And what was he going to tell them, really? They could fuck off about his parents. They knew he was an Indian because he looked like an Indian, and he was August's dad and Buttercup's husband. He spoke English. He could make macaroni. He'd never fired a gun.

He didn't, mostly, drink.

"Can you dance?"

He shrugged. "I can dance at parties."

"Anybody teach you to dance?" This time it was an old guy. Jay tried to remember the last time he'd met an old Indian man, and thought it might have been when he was a tiny kid. This guy looked about a hundred and was probably sixty, and he watched Jay with blanket-heavy seriousness.

"No."

"You wanna learn, you come by my place. Leonard Lachance. I'll teach you to dance. As long as you're not drinking, you understand?"

Jennifer said, in the car, "They're trying to marry you off."

"I'm already married."

"Well. You *were* married. Sort of. No papers, right?" Jay nodded. "So even if she's alive, you don't have to get divorced. You have a job, you're reasonable-looking, you take care of your baby. She needs a car seat, though. Tell Rachel to ask the Band Office. Anyway. Decent Indian guys are like money."

Jay said, "What about the old guy who wants me to dance?"

"Who?"

"Leo or something."

"Leonard wants to teach you to dance?"

"He said."

"You go see him. You smoke?"

"When I'm less broke than I am now."

"Take tobacco anyway."

Jay thought about it and didn't go. The Mennonite store had some decent books. He read most of them, at a dime a book, and gave them back when he was done, and eventually somebody told him to just go get a library card like a normal person, so he did.

In October it got cold, so he learned to clean out the chimney and run the wood stove. Rachel got him chopping wood for her, too. Jay's shoulders filled out. Eventually, he just sprang for the gas and ran a chainsaw. Women found out Jay was chopping wood and suddenly all his days off were full of offers of lunch if he'd work on the pile of mostly dry whole trees lying tangled behind their cabins.

He found animals in the wood piles. Met his first badger, and a skunk that just missed spraying him, and a slow, cold garter snake that Jay looked at for a long time and then gathered up in his pocket. He took it home and showed it to August.

She loved it.

The snake loved the wood stove. It curled up on the floor in the corner, so Jay brought in some medium-sized smooth rocks he found in the river, by the ferry crossing, and used them to make a snake habitat. Rachel stopped by to collect August and nodded.

"Good. They'll hold the heat. You'll need to winterize this place, though. Maybe blankets over the windows and the door. Keep the drafts out."

Two girls came back from Saskatoon and moved in with Rachel. They brought their kids — five between the two of them. Neither of them was interested in Jay, much. "I got other shit to worry about," Megan told him. "And you're not my type. I like butch guys."

Jay went outside in the dark and paused before he got to the outhouse. Nobody awake, and no lights, so he pissed outside. He thought about squatting and then didn't. There was a trick to it — tuck your hand in your jeans careful and kegel down hard, and the stream won't get you wet.

Light-glint when he looked up, and then he did piss on his hand. Swore and wiped it on the frozen grass.

The shining eyes belonged to a porcupine. It was in a poplar tree, about five feet up, and he thought maybe it had been asleep before he pissed on its lawn. It squeaked at him. He went back to bed.

Brent McGowan rolled in from Calgary with a load of gear in his truck, and he got Jay to unload it. Brent wasn't interested in teaching Jay how to work the vacuum tubes, but he had a business computer with actual Internet access, so Jay looked it up. Studied videos. The next time Brent took off, Jay re-built some old lady's radio and she gave him five bucks and some bannock and strawberry jam.

She came back half an hour later and told him to go see Leonard Lachance.

The porcupine was still there, in the yard. It shuffled around, chewing on trees and bits of kids' toys, and annoying Rachel's dogs.

He didn't go see Leonard, but it didn't help. Leonard came by the shop about once every four days, and he brought stuff. Jay wouldn't take the rolled-up cellophane wad of tobacco, though he was careful to be polite about it. He didn't want to learn to dance, or to sweat in the dark, or even to speak Cree, really. Leonard came just to hang out. Jay hadn't realized people still did that, past a certain age.

Days when Jay brought August with him to work, Leonard always knew. He brought her little stuff. Jay checked to make sure it wasn't small enough for her to choke on, and other than that didn't pay attention. She liked the rattle Leonard gave her, even though it was made of wood and something lumpy and looked nothing like a baby toy. August clung to it. When Rachel lifted it out of August's grip, she screamed.

"You gave her this?"

"No, the old guy. Leo."

"Leonard Lachance gave your baby a prayer rattle. S'a good one. He's had that thing my whole life. Gave it to your daughter."

Jay shrugged. Made a note to give it back.

August staggered around the cabin with the rattle. Jay studied her for a long time and realized her toy was made out of a turtle shell. The whole thing, holding something dry inside. When August fell asleep, he put the rattle up high. Twice the porcupine had made it into the cabin, and he didn't think it should be allowed to chew the thing up.

He let Leonard smudge August. Leonard came to Rachel's house with sage and an eagle feather. Said it was for protection. He said prayers over her, and wafted smoke from the smouldering sage-braid over August's head with the eagle feather. Kissed her forehead after and called her *nôsisim*. Went to leave.

Jay said, "You're not going to try to smudge me, too?"

"Sage is for women. I didn't bring sweetgrass." Leonard studied Jay from the door. "Rachel says you'd want sweetgrass. I guess you get to decide for yourself. Come find me if you're ever ready. Try not to start drinking."

❧ ❧ ❧

During the winter, Jay got into reading Norwegian murder mysteries. Or at least, some of them were Norwegian. There was a local craze for the books, and some of them were from Sweden, and some from Denmark. Even more were from Iceland, though when Jay looked it up, Iceland had fewer people than Saskatoon, and it occurred to him that if the Icelanders really got killed off at the rate they were murdered in books, they'd be out of people pretty quick.

On the map, it was so far north. Reykjavik. North of Yellowknife. North of Iqaluit. But not, he realized, as cold. The ocean, somehow, was warmer than the land, so that they were alone in the dark, but less buried than rural Saskatchewan in midwinter. It was something for him to think about. The daylight was short, and he left August at Rachel's most days, because the heat was steady and the TV provided some kind of background noise. Guys had been bringing Rachel meat from their hunting trips, and fish and caribou from up north, and she'd been making traditional food for the kids. Brought it over to Jay's and told him no more sugar for the baby. He could poison himself if he wanted to.

It snowed and the river froze and the ferry came out of the water. He and Jennifer had to drive the long way around to Goose Lake — over an hour — until the ice stabilized. Afterwards, they went over the ice, in the morning dark, while Jay watched for holes and Jennifer told him they'd be fine.

Except, it kept snowing, more than the last three years, Rachel said, and eventually the roads closed and Jay was trapped in Goose Lake. He hiked around the corner to find Jennifer still at the store. She said, "Do you have somewhere to stay?"

He didn't. He went back to work and found Brent in his workshop with the door locked. "Brent?"

"Yeah?"

"Can I come in and talk to you?"

"Not right now. What's up?" Like talking to somebody through the bathroom door. He wondered if Brent tested the sets to make sure they worked by running porn on them or something.

"I'm snowed in. Can I stay here tonight?"

"Isn't there anywhere else you can go?"

"I don't really know anybody. I'll just sack out behind the counter. Keep the bears away."

Brent sighed. Jay could hear it — evidence, he supposed, that if Brent was running porn, the sound was off. Jay said, "Please?"

"Don't make it a habit."

"I won't. Thanks."

Brent let himself out, eventually, and locked the workshop door behind him. Left Jay fixing the ancient radios that piled up while he was sorting them out based on YouTube videos and guesswork. Jay kept the store open. Six o'clock, and then seven o'clock. Just the little neon sign glowing, and the desk light. Dark like Reykjavik. At eight-something, Jennifer let herself in. "Did you find a place?" she asked.

"I'm crashing here. Brent said it was okay."

She shifted on her feet. She had her coat on, and her purse under her arm. "Can I stay too?"

Jay stared at her. "I'm, like, sleeping behind the counter."

"Well, I have an air mattress in the trunk. It's been there since summer, and I think it'll need to be thawed, but it's probably good. We can use that."

She wasn't kidding that it was frozen. Jay stuck it next to the space heater from the back, and the plastic slowly gave until it unfolded. No pump, and Jennifer only looked at him when he pointed that out, so he crouched down and started to blow. It made him dizzy quicker than he expected. The thing was huge — big enough for more than one person — and it was going up too slow. He gave up, plugged the valve, and leaned back. Said, "Your turn," and went to the can.

It was a crappy bathroom, but there was hot water and a couple of actual towels. Jay thought about how long it'd been since he'd last showered, and how close he'd be to Jennifer all night. They had, like, one wool blanket and their coats.

He stripped off and started to wipe himself down. The towels soaked in the plugged sink and gradually absorbed

enough of the dry soap shavings that he could push the layers
of sweat and wood smoke away. He hadn't noticed before, but
in the heat and water, he could smell the smoke-sourness, and
wondered how long he'd been that way. Needed to do better.
He wasn't sure he wasn't the reason that Brent locked himself in the back.

Jennifer knocked. "I gotta pee."

"I'll be a minute."

"I gotta pee *now*."

"I'm mostly naked."

"I've seen it before," she said, and shoved hard enough to
push away Jay's foot holding the door closed and knock him
half over. Scooted past him to the can and pulled down her
jeans, and politely mostly didn't look while Jay scrambled back
into his shorts.

In the dark, under their coats and in all their clothes, Jennifer asked, "So how *did* you get Buttercup pregnant?"

"Buttercup got pregnant the same way everybody does."

"So, not with you."

Jay twisted around. "Fuck off."

"Well, I mean, you used to be a girl. So unless you've got a
lot of money and there's some new lab tricks I don't know
about, she didn't get pregnant with you. So how's August got
your name?"

"Buttercup made them."

"Good trick. Your baby now. Buttercup was smart. And she
picked you, and you seem to be an actual decent human being.
How come you couldn't make her stop hooking?"

"I never made Buttercup do anything."

"She was your woman. Your wife."

"Yeah, but. Like, Buttercup was mine because she said she
was. I was never, ever the boss of her."

Not sure afterwards why he said that, except that Jennifer

sounded like a couple of the girls he'd been in foster homes with: matter-of-fact and just interested. Like she wasn't planning to tell someone, and later she might trade him something good for his honesty.

€ € €

Like an Icelandic murder mystery, the cops eventually showed up. They came out by car, rolling along the dirt roads. Jay stared at them in his cabin and tried to process what they wanted.

"Why can't we stay here?" he said, finally.

"It's easier if we have somebody to write everything down. Record it."

Jay said, "I have a pretty good tape recorder. If you've got a tape we could use..."

"Just come with us, okay? Do you have anybody who can take the baby?" That, *that* he recognized. It was the threat of, *We have people who can take her. Give her to us.* Like he'd never get her back if he let go for a second.

"Her grandma's next door."

The ride into Saskatoon in the car was long, and slow, and lower to the ground than his last run on the bus. They didn't handcuff him, and on the way into the city, they stopped at McDonald's and got him a cheeseburger meal.

He hadn't been eating fast food. It reacted in his stomach like fire and he had to beg for the bathroom as soon as they pulled in on the far side of the city. They gave him a single-room handicapped bathroom, and stood outside while he staggered across to the toilet and got his jeans off just before he shit himself. Tried to remember, while his belly cramped, the last time he'd eaten that much grease at one time.

They were waiting outside, the girl Mountie and the guy.

They took him into a room, and he thought they were going to show him a picture. They wouldn't have brought Buttercup's body all the way to Saskatoon just for identification. But they didn't show him anything. Instead, they gave him a Coke and asked him when was the last time he'd seen his wife, and had they had a fight?

He said he'd told everything to the cops in Winnipeg, when he reported her missing, and no, they hadn't had a fight, and had they found her?

They went around for a while. He wanted them to admit she was dead, and then explain what they wanted, so it took ages for him to figure out they wanted *him* to say she was dead, because then they could ask how he knew that, and then maybe how he'd done it, and if they were lucky, why.

Like on the TV shows: you always ask the husband first. But they were supposed to at least admit she was dead.

Jay said, "I want to talk to an elder."

"You can have a lawyer later. You're not under arrest right now."

"I didn't ask for a lawyer. I want to talk to an elder."

"You have somebody in mind?"

He couldn't think of anyone.

They stayed in the room with him for a long time. They talked about how well he got along with Buttercup. Whether they fought. Whether he knew she was a prostitute. How he felt about it.

He said, "I didn't own her, you know? So she could do what she wanted. She came home every day for supper. It was how I knew she was missing: she didn't come home for dinner. Or breakfast. I told the Winnipeg police right away, and they told me to go home and wait to see if she'd just taken off for a couple of days.

"Buttercup didn't *take off*. She came home drunk sometimes, before she got pregnant, but she always came home. Every single night. She said the guys she hung with when she was drinking started to bug her after a while, and I was better company. And when she found out she was pregnant, she stopped drinking, even.

"We stayed home every night. We watched a lot of TV. She had a friend who made discs of TV shows for her, and we watched them on this old laptop. I was working, so we weren't broke. And she worked at the Claire's downtown. She was pretty. She could sell anybody those little cloth flowers and earrings and stuff.

"She was going to get the baby's ears pierced really soon."

The guy Mountie said, "You're talking about her in the past tense."

"I haven't seen her in eight months. She wouldn't just take off."

"Do you know what happened to her?"

"I told you she was missing!"

He was yelling. He was tired, and his body ached. If they kept this up, he was going to fucking *cry*, and crying was the least manly he ever was.

He said, "Can I go to the can?"

For a second, he thought they weren't going to let him. They were going to make him stay there and piss his pants, or shit himself, depending. Until he confessed to whatever scenario they had in mind. But instead, the guy got up and opened the door and said, "This way."

It wasn't the accessible, one-stall washroom this time. The guy Mountie walked into the men's room behind him, and stood leaning against the old ceramic sinks. Nodded at the urinals.

Jay let himself into one of the stalls. Dropped his jeans and sat down. He had to be careful what he ate. Even McDonald's was giving him the runs. His gut was tied up like he hadn't felt in years.

Since he'd started shots, actually.

Shit.

He grabbed a handful of paper and jammed it between his legs. Hissed when it came away bloody.

He didn't think it had been that long since he'd last had a testosterone shot. He tried to count back, but without the little calendar that Buttercup kept for him, he wasn't sure. At least seven months. Maybe longer.

His tits didn't hurt since he'd had top-half surgery. But just top-half, because the rest was too much work, too expensive, and having invisible parts of himself cut out seemed like too much. He'd had the shots. The other hormones kicked in again when he stopped getting his shots regularly. Making him cry and then bleed and turn back into a fucking *girl*.

Like when he was eleven and got his period the first time, Jay made a pad out of toilet paper. It'd soak through, but not right away. The cheap station paper was too thin, though, and he needed most of the roll to make anything half-workable.

"You okay?"

"I need a sec."

Jay walked out and washed his hands for a long time. Straightened up like his gut didn't hurt.

"Okay. Thanks."

In the room, he asked if they'd found an elder. The girl said, "Don't worry about it for now."

"Can you tell me what happened to Buttercup?"

The girl sighed. "How mad at her were you?"

"I don't get all that mad. Not really." Except for the two fights he'd got into when he started t-shots, but that was years ago.

They went around that for a while. He realized they didn't actually know very much about him. They'd just been told to ask. Like, they knew he and Buttercup were together, but they didn't know anything more complicated than that.

When they gave up and let him out, there was a red smear on the chair and probably a dark spot on his jeans. The girl blinked at him. "You okay?"

"Fine."

"Do you. Um." She looked at him. "Damn." She disappeared into the office and came back a second later. Handed him a yellow-wrapped tampon.

Jay took it and shoved it into his pocket. He didn't say thanks. He said, "Can I go?"

"Sure. We know where to find you."

€ € €

If he'd been a white guy or an obvious college kid, maybe they would have given him a ride home. At least given him a handful of change for the city bus. Or directions to the bus. A suggestion of which bus he needed. Instead, he had to go to the 7-Eleven and ask which way downtown was.

So fucking cold. He had a coat, but no gloves or boots. It was a long way just to get to the river, and then he was exposed to the full smash of the wind. Like getting kicked. It helped, though, with the pain in his gut. Enough that he spotted the art gallery on the other bank and made a beeline for it. Dodged the chary security woman and went downstairs to the can. Messed up pad out, tampon in.

Fucking body.

He needed to find a doctor. An endocrinologist. He had no idea where to start, in a strange city, in a province he didn't have a health card for. He didn't think they took walk-ins.

The hospital loomed glassy and white on his windward side, but he didn't think they'd see him as an emergency. He went anyway.

It took a while to find the urgent care doors: the building was a zig-zagging maze. The nurse stared him down. He said, "My gut hurts." Nothing else.

They triaged him so low he might have to wait for days, but it was out of the wind, and he didn't think they'd actively make him leave. Whatever hospital he'd picked, though, was the wrong one. This was, he understood, getting to be a nice neighbourhood, and he'd have blended in more at another one.

He was there eight hours. Two major accidents came through, and a fair number of people who'd had heart attacks or falls. An elder came in with a bad foot, and she watched him for a while while she waited too. Gave him a sip of her tea when she got some.

Nobody checked on him. He wondered if they were waiting for him to leave.

His gut hurt so much. The tampon had soaked through. He made a new pad in the toilet.

Walked out, finally, into the neighbourhood of big trees and brick buildings that looked vaguely like a *Sesame Street* set. Pretty, even at night. It didn't look expensive, exactly. More like the place he'd lived with Buttercup when they first got together. It was enough to make him stand still. Imagine if he turned just right, he could go home.

He opened his eyes. It was dark. He wasn't entirely sure how late. He started walking west.

It took him another hour to find the Friendship Centre. He had to walk completely around the downtown, and he was bone-cold. His toes felt like a small flap of skin had grown in, sliding between his foot and the toes proper so that his toes became their own bone-cored units that could slide away if he lost his footing. His hands were red inside his pockets. His face was raw.

It wasn't the soup-kitchen kind of centre that he'd been hoping for, but they let him use the phone. He left a message for Rachel, that he was stuck in the city. That he was working on it.

He had no idea how long it might be before she called him back.

He was hungry and freezing cold. His whole body hurt.

If he could just fix the hormone problem, it would be something.

He went outside like he was going to smoke. Found the alley and dug around in a trash bin.

He'd have preferred glass. It was easy to break, easy to deal with, but then he remembered that in Saskatchewan, you could return bottles for money, so all the garbage had been picked over.

He was left with metal. He found a can that had been somebody's lunch. Dug again until he found the lid. It was some kind of sharp.

He didn't actually cut himself until he was a block from the hospital. Sat down on the snowbank for a while and thought about it. Then rubbed the lid off in the snow, pulled off his jacket to keep it clean, and gouged the metal edge hard into his forearm.

He wasn't stupid. He avoided most of the veins, and all the tendons he could see.

When he walked back into urgent care with a hand wrapped around his shredded skin, they were a lot more interested in him. They stuck him in a bed almost immediately.

They put him on a 72-hour hold, and had him moved to the University Hospital. It took most of his assessment period to get referred to an endocrinologist.

The resident came in, sleepy, while Jay was still on the secure floor. Bitched at him while she went over his body. He didn't come with health records, only his top-half surgery and his bleeding lowers. She took away his blood, and twelve hours later came back, gave him a couple of shots, and told them to release him. Referred him for out-patient care.

Rachel didn't pick him up. Somebody else.

He tried to remember the girl's name. He'd kissed her at a party. The shawl dancer.

"Amber," she said. "Get in."

She took him back to Almighty Voice on secondary roads. The pavement was broken, intermittently, and he realized they went this way because there were fewer patrols and she didn't have a lot of faith that she'd pass vehicle inspection if they were pulled over. The heater worked, though. It blasted him from bone-chill into nausea, and he rode home low in the car, staring at flat white fields with extra stubble in them pushing up through the snow crust.

He was vaguely aware that his bad mood was at least in part the testosterone working its way back through his system. He'd run all the way over to girl and back to man in the course of a single biochemical week, and his brain had to go through some sort of hormonal primal-scream therapy before he was going to recognize his own psyche again. Best to say nothing. Amber pulled into her own yard and let him out. Jay's door handle didn't work, so he had to wait for her to do it.

"You can stay with me for a couple of days."

"I gotta go see my baby."

"She's okay. Mrs. McLeod has her. You maybe could have thought about her before you cut yourself up, but. Well. Anyway, when your crazy eyes settle down, I'll give you a ride over there and you can talk to Mrs. McLeod about what you're going to do."

Amber set up an air mattress for him on her floor. It was the kind you floated on a lake on, sort of narrow, but it didn't hurt him when he lay down on it. He slept away the rest of his tranquilizers, and woke up to an almost-empty house. The lady watching TV, he thought, might be Amber's mom. She waved at him.

He went outside and found a chainsaw. Cut up all the logs he could find and thought about going into the bush for dead trees. Gave up because he didn't have real boots. He took the wood back into the house and gave himself a sponge bath in the can. Two guys came in and made mac and cheese, and shared some with him. One of them gave Jay a beer.

"You the guy who fixes radios?"

He fixed the tape player on the one guy's truck. He was Mike Redbird. Buttercup's aunt's ex-boyfriend. They drove around the reserve for a while, then into the little French-language town where they had this amazing poutine in the cultural centre. They split an order in the truck's cab.

Mike said, "Do you know how to hunt?"

Jay shook his head. Sucked smoked meat and gravy off the fry he was eating.

"I'll show you sometime."

They didn't go see Rachel. Instead, Mike took Jay to his place and introduced him to the chore team: these rangy brown horses that looked like they'd come out of the hills, but fast-looking and tall. Mike's dad and uncles ran on the chuckwagon circuit in the summers. Mike had had a couple of bad wrecks and quit, but he still used horses to clear brush and move hay. "It's quieter than a tractor, and you don't need to buy gas to start them up in the morning."

Mike had a couple dozen little cows that he was feeding over the winter. His back yard was full of frozen cow shit, and the fence was held together with orange twine, but the cows didn't look like they were going anywhere. They bunched up together in the three-sided shelter of grey boards. Bumped against Mike when he went in to check them.

Jay stayed there for a couple of days. They played Xbox, and Mike told him stories about Buttercup's stint as a rodeo groupie when she was just about thirteen that only lasted until Mike got her a horse of her own.

They got drunk together, and Mike told him how Shayleigh, Buttercup's aunt, Mike's ex, got killed in Vancouver, six years ago.

Jay said, "How many?"

"Of the girls in Mrs. McLeod's family? Five. Six if you count Buttercup's mom, but we don't actually know what happened to her. She just took off."

"I didn't hurt Buttercup."

"I didn't think you did. But she's dead. You know that, right?"

"Cops think I killed her."

"*Thought* you killed her. You aren't in jail, are you?"

⋘ ⋘ ⋘

Brent gave Jay this long stare when he came back to work. It went all the way over Jay's hormone-wrecked body and down his arms past the edges of his T-shirt to the patchy bandages covering the mess of his wrists. He said, "You're a mess. So nobody will believe you, no matter what you told them. So you might as well come see."

Jay followed him into the workshop. Brent locked the front door, first, and turned the sign to *Closed*. In the back, he had a couple of bright flood-lights that stripped all the shadows from the world, so that everything was hyper-detailed, and the dust stood out in each TV cabinet's ornamental grooves.

Brent showed him how to open up those cabinets. Pull the guts out of the old TVs like you were cleaning eavestroughs, or gutting a moose. Jay went through the parts on the old trestle-table, separating still-working pieces from the irreparably dead.

The working parts, Brent told him, went into clear plastic shoe-boxes. Jay had a dozen of those up front, for piece-work.

While Jay watched, Brent skinned a new flat-panel TV, still sporting its Wal-Mart stickers, out of its cardboard and fitted it in behind the warped glass of the TV cabinet. Hooked a cable-adapter up to the back. Through the dirty glass of the old screen, it looked like the shows Jay remembered as a kid. The shape of it cut off the wide-aspect parts of the broadcast, and curved the edges, real retro-nostalgic shit.

He worked with Brent most of the afternoon. They added a couple of sheets of plastic to help with the colour balance. Then, while Jay braced the flat-screen's protective shell, Brent added old bricks, pieces of concrete, and occasionally rocks, measuring the whole thing on an industrial scale until the resulting cabinet, including lid, weighed exactly what the old one had. Glued it all into place.

He added additional hook-ups to the back of the cabinet and ran connectors through to the flat-screen so that it all linked up. Secured everything with a spray of clear silicone.

Jay said, sometime after dark, "Do you do that for the local ones, too?"

"Not yet. Not until we get digital signals up here. Until then, we have the extra parts." Brent nodded at the shoeboxes of salvage.

They wrote up the invoice for service together. It went to Calgary. Total cost of retrofit for digital signal, eight thousand sixty-eight dollars, plus GST. Plus PST. Plus shipping.

Jay stared at it. The receipts lying around for the flat-screens suggested they cost about $150 apiece.

Brent said, "I haven't had any complaints." He handed Jay the boxes of old TV guts to carry up to the front. "Try not to break those. It's a limited supply."

❦ ❦ ❦

Rachel let him see August practically every day. She'd learned a bunch of new words while he was in the city. She called him *daddy*.

She called Rachel *mommy*.

Rachel was making August a jingle-dress, though, and teaching her to dance, and he couldn't argue with that.

When he checked it, the cabin was freezing cold. Jay took his stuff and went to stay at Mike's. Amber came by some nights and they played Xbox together. She made him chili. He went back to her place and fixed her mom's TV. It was one of Brent's projects, keeping the regional televisions running until the next technological shift. He billed cheap, because the elders brought him jam and bannock, and he liked that shit almost as much as he liked the cabinets on the TV sets they kept shipping him.

And Jay didn't have a status card, but Mike said as long as

they stayed on-reserve, no one would give him shit about his hunting rights. They practiced for a while with an ancient rifle out behind Mike's place, away from the cows, until Jay could hit little sketched targets on the trees.

Then they went out into the bush. Cut logs first, and hauled them out with the horses to points where people with decent trucks could collect them. Stayed at Mike's grandpa's trapping cabin, and drank most nights. It got dark so early. They ran the wood stove and read and swore at each other, and when Mike came in while Jay was stripped down, he didn't say anything about it.

The animals moving around the cabin were so *quiet*. Mike showed Jay their tracks, and they took the rifle and a knife and followed.

The porcupine in the tree was probably a different one. Jay looked at it, up in the brushy tangle, and didn't say, *That's Buttercup.*

Mike pointed out the deer nibbling on dry grass on the edge of a field.

Jay looked down the rifle for a long time, trying to sight it properly. He aimed for the deep body, breathing out. Shifted at the last second and brought his sight up to the deer's eye before he fired.

Man Gave Names to All the Animals

THE APARTMENT IS MOSTLY EMPTY AND NOT VERY warm, so over the weekend she moves the goldfish into the bathtub.

She's alone. Or, well. Jacob isn't gone, exactly. He hasn't vanished, or died. He only decided to go walkabout, and then, once he found himself, he decided to couch-surf for a while in Vancouver. It's warmer there; she understands. And he found a job, too, on the edge of almost-gentrified East Hastings, working in a store that sells clothing projects, every piece made in a single day by a single artist somewhere in the city. The place has a certain amount of local cachet. They have a trade in asymmetrical vests and sketchily embroidered leggings. Deconstructed shorts, to be worn over base-layers by the snowboarders at Whistler.

He emails her that he's sketching new designs. He has this idea for quick-creation T-shirts. He can sew the jersey together and then paint images of animals right onto the fabric, skip the mass-production silk-screening process entirely. They're going to let him try, maybe next month. In the meantime, he's modelling for them. Jacob doesn't send her pictures, but they're blogged by the store: Instagram-filtered snaps of her waifish, overgrown boy in layered clothes. He climbs over logs on Kitsilano beach in hand-sewn raw denim. Lolls in a shredded silk scarf on a playground in what might be Burnaby. They were going for mid-America, she thinks, and missed.

The marginal banner-image of the site shows Jacob in soft, green army jeans in the old, almost-closed Chinatown. He's grown a beard, just a thin one, and he might be wearing eyeliner.

She has to follow multiple links to reach the shots of him modelling underwear in someone's retro basement. Purple jockey shorts with red piping on them, knitted socks, and apparently nothing else cover him up in a dirty shower stall.

It's sexy, in an overdone, quasi-American Apparel way. The project's site states explicitly that they intend to exploit only male bodies in the course of their advertising.

Jacob looks stunningly good in a modest slip-dress and tights. On his bare shoulder, someone's written *I'm the toughest girl I know* in sharpie.

He's happy, most likely, but he left her with this apartment in Winnipeg, two bedrooms where she can only afford one, and a crawling menagerie in residence around his floor-mattress. The terrariums host spiders and small lizards. Along the ceiling there's a Habitrail of feral mice, each dressed in a small waistcoat Jacob sewed for it. The goldfish bump at their tank glass whenever she approaches.

She wants to tell Jacob to go screw himself and let the menagerie die, but. They're animals. It's not in any way their fault that they were captured by a ridiculous man-thing with a mania for shoplifting and a tendency to flee the city when his credit card bills arrive. Most of what Jacob owns is salvaged out of dumpsters, but then he'd come home with a cashmere overcoat from the boutiqued second floor of the downtown Bay, and handmade shoes. He'd fill up their fridge with Italian pickles from De Luca's and bloody-fresh raw meat, and commence cooking. He stole cheeses. He couldn't resist the brie wheels from the warehouse where he ostensibly worked. She came home most nights when he was still around to find him eating finger-sized slices of triple-cream.

His credit card bills demand sums of four and five figures. He left them piled on the kitchen table next to his note, *Gone to Vancouver. Feed the fish*. On the back: *please*.

It's winter all over Canada, but deepest on the prairies. Pipes are bursting in Osborne Village: too many students cramming their hot showers into plumbing installed at the turn of the last century. The resident freaks are almost invisible, wrapped in scarves and layers of toques.

Pinky waves up at her from the street. He has three hats over his shaved scalp; you'd never know he's tattooed from his forehead to the base of his spine.

€ € €

She met Jacob when they were both working at Safeway. She was learning to shave the sweet, dense deli meats into onion-skin-translucent fragments. Her trainer left to take a smoke break, and while he was gone she slipped and shaved the thinnest layer of skin off her left hand. A moment existed when there wasn't even any pain, while blood pooled slowly in her palm like it was raining. She stared at it. Nauseated, suddenly, by the ham-smell and the awareness of her own flesh. Blood all over the deli's back room. And there were customers waiting, out front, wanting artisan sandwiches and breakfast samosas, and she was bleeding.

This sudden, bright instant in which it hurt *so much* followed.

She wrapped her hand in an entire roll of paper towels. Bolted out past the waiting villagers and ran for the back of the store.

Jacob was stealing cheese. He was off-shift, stuffing hard Italian cheeses from the bridge into the pockets of his too-big pants. Turned around like he didn't even care, and looked at her.

"Oh wow," he said. "That's soaking through." It was. She was going to die of blood loss. They could ship her body out to some suburb for processing and then return her to the deli as food.

She hadn't told the supervisor about the layer of her skin left in the shaved ham.

Jacob looked her over, and then he wrapped his jacket around her hand and dragged her out on the loading dock. Jumped, pulling her after him. Hailed them a cab on Roslyn Road and took her to Misericordia Urgent Care to have her too-open palm closed up again.

They did it with superglue. Jacob thought it was amazing.

The next day at work, he brought her a sandwich where she was checking groceries with one hand wrapped in gauze. Panini with pesto and soft white melted cheese.

He said, "It's safe. It's turkey." And stuck a sealed deli bag into the pocket of her apron. She opened it later, at home, and inside the layers of waxed paper there was ham, and blood, and what could only be her skin. Jacob came knocking after dark with a bottle of purple-sweet Baby Duck wine, and they buried her dead flesh on the river bank. He said he was gay, sort of but not really, and he liked breasts, and she kissed him. Pulled his hair a little to make him whimper.

❧ ❧ ❧

Jacob was — is — half her size. He's this tiny, impossible boy-man with benign sociopathic tendencies and she's ... not. She's vicious in her own way, and she likes it when he moans, and she steals his comics and never tells him where they went. On a half dozen afternoons, she slept with him. When he needed a roommate and she needed a lease, they picked up this sixties-banal apartment within walking distance of work.

She learned that he kept a very, very clean bathroom. That his clothes were all carefully catalogued by origin: Value Village, other thrift source, accepted from church donation bin, stolen from church donation bin, stolen from co-workers, stolen from shopping malls, purchased by his parents, left over from high school, given to him by exes. A small selection of bought-and-paid-for, near-couture pieces hung wrapped in plastic dry-cleaning bags in one corner. He only wore them when he was depressed and drinking.

He only smoked pot when he was pretending to be home-less. Once he slept for two nights under the Osborne Bridge. He came back every time he needed to use the toilet, then left again, still reeking of smoke.

Jacob walked out on Safeway and went to work at a central grocery warehouse, for reasons she can only assume were cheese-related. She got a better job, managing an Indian im-port shop at the Forks Market. Old buildings, restored for the sacred purpose of downtown revitalization, were converted into inexpensive boutique shops, art galleries, and artisan-style single-food retailers. Working there meant she could shed her most professional layer. Burn her polyester work pants in the winter snow. Draw on her arms with henna.

She sold a lot of henna in the week after that, to high

school girls mostly. Showed them how to draw on themselves. Baby lesbians came in and bought henna for each other and drew on each other's camisoled backs in the food court.

And then Jacob took off. He left the note, his credit card bills, and a bag of swedish gummy fish on her bed. There was a top-of-the-line espresso maker still in its box in the kitchen. He'd burned the receipt in the sink so she couldn't return it. Sharpied on the box, it said, *Guerilla barista training will take you farther than a BFA, grasshopper. Learn to mix it with chai for increased karma and serenity.*

€ € €

Chai lattes keep her warm when the window seals give out and the cold seeps in. She needs to buy caulking, big tubes of silicone to push the winter back out, but the nearest actual hardware store is an hour and three bus transfers away, in a mega-box complex in deepest suburbia. Most nights, she's too tired to think about making the trek. She makes hot drinks for herself and steams milk for the animals. Gathers the touchable ones close to her while she watches *Lost*.

Damn Jacob for running away to the boreal rain world without her. For leaving her with the fur-children.

The peripherals on Jacob's fish tank fail slowly, one at a time, and the tank greens in the cold. She carries the fish one at a time, in coffee mugs, into the bathroom and lets them swim in the warmer, cleaner bath-water. Leaves them there when they spread out in the porcelain space and wag their fish-tails.

The warm bathwater's a better heat source than the forced air vents in the living room, so she moves into the bathroom too. Makes herself a nest of blankets and towels and opens Jacob's credit card bills.

The things he bought might well have been random, though he organized their purchase with an accountant's precision. One bill's almost entirely for groceries that never came home; another's for designer clothes she's only ever seen on Chinese-mainland-born university students. One lists only unhelpfully-named web businesses which, when she looks them up, all sell some variation on high-end, ethically-sourced bondage gear.

The guinea pig scrambles into the steam-warmed bathroom and burrows into the clothing and soft flesh on her belly. It's hungry. All the produce in the refrigerator is liquid, possibly toxic. Nothing edible for woman or tiny beast. The mice will eat pellets. The fish eat desiccated flakes of other fish. The lizards eat freeze-dried meal worms. Jacob left supplies for all of the animals; it's only that she hasn't been shopping for a while. She gets nearly-off bananas from the market at work, eats leftover cheese and frozen chicken fingers at home, and cereal. She'd thought there were enough apples and carrots to get the tiny pig through the week. There aren't.

She wraps the animal up in her parka and goes to find Pinky.

Pinky isn't home, but he almost never is, at least when she needs him. He occupies a third floor bachelor suite in one of the sister-buildings across the alley. Wanders around at night picking fights with gutter punks in the summer. In the winter . . . she doesn't know. He goes out. Lurks in bus shelters downtown. Eats children. But he gave her the punch code to the building's main doors years ago, so at least she can settle in the hall to wait. Smell the faint mist of bacon and blue wall-to-wall carpet that the building radiates.

It's possible the thin blue-green algae layer growing on the cinderblock wall, down near the carpet, is guinea pig nutritious. The pig isn't sure. It sniffs at the growth for a while, then shrugs its off-centre fur body and crawls back into her lap.

Later, after it's dark, Pinky says, "Did you want something?"

⇜ ⇜ ⇜

His apartment is home to a massive gaming system, one enormous lounge chair/bed, and almost nothing in the way of clothes. She'd visit more often, but Pinky's dedicated to nudity, and while he's not that hard to look at, there's nowhere for her to sit except the floor. It puts her on dick-level when he's curled up in the lounger. He's protective of the chair, too. It has a name and a complicated personal history. She must have looked miserable in the hallway, because he doesn't object when she sits down on its microfiber end, but nods and goes about stripping off his clothes and throwing them out of the kitchen.

Pinky cooks naked. He claims that's why he's vegan. Hot, spattering animal fat would scar him in ways he doesn't want to consider. In practice, this means he eats ramen noodles and salads. The place looks like it. He doesn't. He looks like he eats the flesh of devout elderly women.

He's a huge guy, tattooed all over and almost hairless. He has scars on his back that suggest he spent his formative years in high-seas piracy. Unreasonably sharp teeth, which he may have had done cosmetically, or possibly did himself. Wrapped in his winter layers, he looks unapproachably homeless, and possibly psychotic. Naked, he looks queer, and kinky, and unexpectedly asexual.

From the kitchen he calls, "Send it in here. The pig."

"Why?"

"I found a peach at the back of the fridge."

She can smell it. She shouldn't be able to, not cold as it is, but the flesh is soft enough, or he's held it in the steam of the boiling ramen water, and suddenly there's fruit sugar all over the room, and the pig's electric, scrambling out of her arms and dashing for its dinner.

Pinky brings her ramen noodles mixed with tofu and bok choy. The waft of packaged MSG flavouring is almost overwhelming, but it still smells like food. She drops to the floor, takes the disposable chopsticks he offers, and eats. Watches while Pinky folds himself around his bowl of noodles and soy protein. While he plays *Mass Effect 2*, systematically slaughtering insectile gang members. She falls into the story, eventually. It's a kind of zen-state, watching him play: her brain accepts the long loops of repeated background while the avatar kills and re-kills the digital people in his path. They crawl after him if he doesn't properly finish them off. It's pretty.

She falls asleep again. She needs coffee, real coffee, but she's been subsisting on decaf and her brain is shutting down. All her world is cold and wet and full of animals.

Pinky wakes her up with a shake. He says, "Go home and sleep properly. Maybe leave the guinea pig with me." The pig has climbed up on the chair with him, presumably right over her sleeping body. Little animal curled up on Pinky's tattooed thigh, just below his dick.

On her way out, Pinky says, "If you really want to get rid of the mice, Gary has snakes. Like, about six of them."

She doesn't remember that until she's at work the next day, shelving a box of rough-carved weeping Buddha figurines. Thinks about the mice, rapid and tiny and nattily dressed. They're starting to smell. Jacob cleaned their cages and trails out semi-regularly, usually when she wasn't home, because the mice weren't her first choice for roommates. They could go; they could be useful. Save Gary a few dollars at the pet store.

Only, there's this problem where she doesn't think of them as food. They're living animals, all skin and fur and bright eyes. They have nothing in common with roast beef or sundried tomato smoked chicken loaf, or gypsy salami.

Meat's not always distinguishable from her own hands, but she convinces herself that doesn't mean it's made of animals. It couldn't be. They're so alive. Busy. Talking to each other in the night.

She can't keep them all. The smell's locking up her lungs.

❦ ❦ ❦

The fetish people come, and they take care of all of it. Some of them bring her food, too.

Gary borrows her apartment key and removes the mice, then hugs her when he brings the key back. His glasses are slightly dusty from the promised clean-up of a dozen delicious mice with Habitrail. She gets a clean apartment and reinforcement of her relationship with this kinky bastard who fixed things with the telecoms so she can afford high-speed Internet access on a shop-slave's wages.

Gary works in tech support, sometimes in accounts. He just altered her plan a little, so that she pays on some beautiful introductory deal forever.

He and Pinky have the same mistress. Dana. She manages a hair salon in St. Boniface.

Dana sends her a thank-you note. They used to be her snakes, before snakes were banned from her apartment complex. She says she thinks it wasn't about the snakes, not really, but you can't make regulations against suspiciously dominatrix-like behaviour among consenting adults, so they took her snakes away.

They didn't, it seems, ban lizards. Just snakes. The rules were oddly clear on that.

Dana comes over three nights later and leaves with two terrariums and a hot rock. She brings a friend who likes spiders. They're tattooed all over her arms. It's what she does, body art, and the spiders — the live ones — are for the new shop. They'll live out their lives in exquisitely clean glass cages, studied by college girls looking for basic lower-back flash and the fetish-scene people working on full-body pieces.

When they're gone, she pulls out her phone and takes pictures of Jacob's empty room. Nothing left but the fish in the bathtub. She warms the water up periodically, though not from the tap. Everything the fish get has been passed twice through a Brita filter and then heated gently on the stove. In their new, larger space, the fish are growing. She put in a plastic castle for them to look at.

The fish crap clinging to the porcelain is a bit gross. And she desperately needs a shower. Two weeks of sponge baths and washing her hair in the sink have reduced her to a homeless look rivalling Pinky's. The goth girls at the market are a bit afraid of her now. She wishes she could send the smell of herself to Jacob along with the pictures of his absent pets. Instead, she takes naked pictures of her grimy self, perched on the tub's edge.

Jacob sends her back a set of non-commercial photos he's done. Maybe he was always fated to be some kind of fetish model, curious and lazy and always in search of the prettiest possible scenario for his cheerful perversions. He loved the sight of her blood that first day. It's a wonder he didn't come on the spot.

€ € €

His cellphone was left behind under his bedding. When she drags the mattress out to the curb, she finds the phone, recharges it, and collection agencies start calling.

Yes, this is his phone. No, he's gone.

No, she doesn't know where he is. Not really. He might have gone over the border by now and joined the thriving Seattle kink scene. Maybe they should look for him on niche Internet pay-sites.

She throws the cellphone into the bathtub eventually. For a second she thinks this will solve her fish problem, but all that happens is that the phone becomes fatally waterlogged. At least it's quiet.

It's possible some vicious part of her brain means to do it, though, when she knocks an open bottle of shampoo into the tub while she's washing her hair.

The shampoo is vegan and biodegradable, but in that concentration, it's not good for fish. Still, she manages to rescue six of them by scooping them out with her cupped hands, rinsing them quickly under the sink tap, and then dropping them into a floor-mopping bucket filled half with tap water, half by the kitchen water filter. The fish stagger-swim around their blue plastic prison, looking drugged.

She flushes the dead. She rinses her hair in the shower. The worst of the fish mess washes right off the porcelain when she aims the stream with her hands.

Still, it makes her cry. The fish were innocent. They were beautiful. Big, spotted creatures, carp from a warm, clear climate just trying to survive in the Winnipeg winter. She wanted them to go away, but she didn't want them to die.

She phones Pinky. He comes over.

She doesn't ask him what he does with the bucket of gold-fish. It's only important to her that someone with a commitment to animal survival surpassing PETA's should be the person who takes them away. She doesn't think Pinky would do anything terrible to her goldfish. Not really. At worst, he might locate some corporate atrium with a fountain and release them into the wild. Let them nibble on the fingers of certified accountants having lunch and scare them into dropping their tuna sandwiches.

Delicious.

Just before the end of February, Pinky moves in. It takes him two hours. Fetish people come out to help him carry the epic chair and his television. Tiny girls she's only ever seen in stiletto heels and corsets show up in boots and jeans and carry grocery bags full of Pinky's clothes over. She didn't realize he had so many. They invade the kitchen and start a sweet potato curry cooking, and two big guys wearing collars take over minding it when the girls go out. They fondle her kitchen a little, but they're clean and careful, and they sharpen all the secondhand knives from her drawers while they're working.

Gary comes in carrying the guinea pig in the pocket of his oversized coat.

She doesn't know when these became her people. She met most of them through Pinky, before she met Jacob, when she was the lost girl uncomfortable in a hipster neighbourhood. She just wanted to find people a little less self-consciously twee. She isn't sure she did. But. Pinky wraps himself in tiny, glittering thongs and his overcoat and goes out to parties and brings people back in the small hours of the morning to get quietly high with and listen to vintage records together. Over time, they've assembled an entire sixties hi-fi out of thrift store finds and garage sale hunting.

They carry the hi-fi into her apartment piece by piece, setting it up in the terrarium-vacated living room.

Dana sets the turntable to play imported British trip-hop vinyl.

She curls up in Pinky's chair while the others are sitting on the floor, engaged in an apparently epic and pre-planned Dungeons & Dragons game. She learns that Gary has a gaming bag identical to his bondage bag. It's full of manuals and hand-painted pewter figures, and a pair of wrist cuffs that were stuffed into the wrong sack at some point in the distant past and then became part of his standard gaming gear. He has the cuffs on and the guinea pig in his lap.

Twelve-sided dice roll. Tiny figures move through an invisible world. Someone brought along a set of pewter rat-soldiers vaguely reminiscent of *The Nutcracker*. One of Dana's figures is a snake goddess.

Pinky, at some point in the intervening time since she last saw him naked, has had a small school of goldfish tattooed onto his rib cage. Some of them have lost scales, and underneath they're clearly run by clockwork.

She wants that tattoo. Maybe he'll draw it on her if she asks.

Reaches out to ask him, but he only takes her scarred hand, kisses it, and hands her the guinea pig. It nuzzles in like it remembers her as the only bright point in an earlier, darker life. It might only love her body wash. After the fish left, the bathroom still smelled so much like them that she gave in and bought a bag full of cheap fruit-scented bath products. Still, she doesn't think the pig's ever going to leave her again. It's burrowed down inside her shirt, and it lies there, curled up just below her breasts, twitching as it dreams.

Parrothead

1.

YOU'RE LUCKY, YOUR MOM SAYS, THAT AS A GROUP you — meaning you and her, and also your sisters — can pull off a brush cut. Without looking too dykey, is what she says, exactly. Red wine in her hand in a champagne flute that says *Swanson Grad '90*. "You girls got my face," she says. "To go with my shoulders. Even when we've cut our hair short, it doesn't look butch.

"More Amazonian. We're big women. A bit scary, but men like it. They come around to it and then they realize they like the raw bones."

"I carried your father to bed, a couple of times."

She picked up *dykey* from your sister Bernie, whose short-lived lesbian period played out in Fort McMurray, up north in Alberta. Bernie went up there with some boyfriend. He washed dishes and she got a job driving trucks in the tar sands. It didn't sound like her, but she told you once on the phone that she was doing recon for possible eco-terrorist purposes, only they didn't pan out. And you think she liked the work. She took machine shop one term in high school, to mess with people, and discovered she liked diesel engines.

Eventually Bernie met this woman and the two of them lived together for eight months or so in a basement bachelor suite. Bernie has hung out with lesbians her whole life, so your mom didn't notice. After, when Bernie talked it through with her on the phone, she said, "I've looked a bit dykey my whole life. Chicks keep trying to pick me up. I wanted to check if they were on to something."

"You don't look dykey," your mom said. "You just look like me."

Bernie and your mom and your sister May are all over six feet tall and genuinely big-boned. They look fat, wear size ten or twelve, even when they're underweight. Your sisters still have their long, wire-straight hair, and all their lives they've looked like 1970s stoner throwbacks.

Your mom cut her top-knot tangle into a brush cut in 1989, when she saw it in a magazine and liked it on the model. She pairs the look with her usual long skirts and T-shirts. When brush cuts shifted into pixie cuts, she didn't bother learning to re-style it.

You got most of that — her style, her bones — but missed the height. People look at you and think you're tall because you look like your mom, and then guys blink when you still tuck under their chins. Not even quite five foot six. Too tall to tuck up like that on your dad, but you inherited his glass shins and duck feet to prove you're his.

So when you go out running, you mostly do it at night, when no one can see you flail.

Since you moved in with your mom, you run on the gravel roads after dark, or early in the morning if you can't sleep. You watch for cars. Step into the ditch as soon as you see headlights and crouch there until they pass. Try to get your breath back.

The times you've skipped crouching, the trucks always

stopped and offered you a ride. They ask if you're alright. You didn't recognize any of them, these neighbours in vehicles, but they all know who you are. They ask if your mom's okay.

One offered you his cellphone. Said you could keep it for a few days and he'd swing by and pick it up early next week. He looked like some asshole who beat you up in middle school, though you couldn't remember his specific name, so you told him you had a phone. Thanks. You were just out for some air.

"I thought you'd be more into yoga."

"I do it sometimes."

This weird moment you thought he'd suggest you teach a class in it. Maybe at his church. So, to stop him, you said, "How's your wife?"

It shut him down. You did a stranger-danger rapid step back from the truck and told him to take care.

He waves, though, when he drives past, even now. He's going to force you to run on the deer trails in the pasture.

You don't want to meet up with *people* all the time. It's why you moved in with your mom.

You should tell her, soon, that you're pregnant, but at four months, it's not showing, and you're sort of curious to see how far *big-boned* can carry you.

2.

There are jokes about moving back in with your parents, but none of them really fit. You can't move *back* in with them, because there's no *them*, and only a partial *back*. Your father and mom decided when you were a teenager that they'd run their course, and you actually lived with your dad after their split. Watched him quit smoking and learn to ballroom dance. You picked up his cigarettes for trade and then started smoking them yourself. Six years until you quit. Now you can't find the bottoms of your lungs even when you road-run every day for a week, and you should tell him that, make him feel guilty and maybe lend you the money for a mid-range humidifier for your bedroom, or a car that runs at least three days a week.

This house is the one you all only lived in until you were ten, when May and Bernie moved out. It's the house where you found your parents' fully illustrated *The Joy of Sex* and your mom's Harold Robbins books.

You were so clinical about it. Found an X-acto knife and carefully razored sex-scene pages out of the paperbacks and traded them to boys on your school bus for their Cheez Whiz sandwiches and tapes of The Doors.

This is the part your mom forgets — that you were only ten that last year. She forgets because Bernie's eight years older than you, and May's ten. You should have been the baby of the family. Instead, by the time you were old enough to listen in a real way to adults, they were bored with baby talk and simply included you in their conversations.

It meant you were the little girl who knew a dozen elaborately dirty jokes but not a single one about elephants.

You told the jokes you knew, and somebody tattled on you, and the evangelical pastor came to your house and talked to your parents about how it was *inappropriate*, and didn't it alarm them that a little girl had such an *explicit* vocabulary?

It was, he said, one of the signs.

Signs of — you still remember this — Satanism. He was on some kind of kick about the need to watch out for cults. Satanic cults. He clarified that after your mom asked how out there a church had to be, exactly, before it turned into a *cult*. Would his church count, for instance?

He left a bunch of pamphlets that you collected. They're in the wall of the room that used to be yours. When you were clearing a space for your bed, you found the loose panel along the floor moulding and behind it were the warnings about Satanism, and your unsold sex scenes, and a bunch of half-finished friendship bracelets that you made for the girls at neo-pagan day camp.

You'd asked if you could please join a cult, and your father said you couldn't, but your mom said you could try being a witch, if you wanted to.

It didn't entirely stick, but you stayed just Wiccan enough to find covens in every town you've ever lived except Swanson, because your mom asked you not to mention the day camp at school. When your parents left this house and moved you into Saskatoon, the Wiccans found you. Made you one of them. You became one of the circle of black-clad girls lurking in the shadows of Joni Mitchell Collegiate, terrorizing the missionary kids.

3.

Your mom stands in the door of your old room. She says, "I'm going back to bed, honey. Feed yourself?"

"Sure."

She took over Bernie and May's old room when she moved back here. She has a mattress in there, and bunch of afghans and quilts from her last place in the city, and an old TV and VCR. Bootleg tapes of C-list action shows from early 90s cable crowd against her sleeping zone. They're balanced by slews of romance novels. Those and your father's computer, circa 2001.

It's a crap machine, but that doesn't really matter since the only Internet out here is dial-up. You pick up the phone at night and it screams because she's logged into some retro low-bandwidth chat system.

You don't know who she talks to, but she does it all night.

She sleeps until two in the afternoon and then comes down to find coffee and multigrain toast. Takes a handful of vitamins. Completely fails to sort through the increasingly filthy file boxes piled in the living room that hold a decade's worth of tax returns and the mortal remains of her career.

If there's wine, she drinks it. Then she goes back upstairs. Sometimes in the middle of the night you hear her taking a shower.

And you guess she can do what she likes, since she's retired. It was early retirement, though, and it means she's only on half-pension. It's a problem. Since your EI ran out, you have even less money than she does. But she'd moved back into this house before you joined her, and the neighbours who bought it when you left are giving her some kind of break on the rent. They didn't really want the house, after all, just the land. It's surrounded by brushy pasture and hay fields that haven't been cut and swarm with mosquitoes.

It isn't your mom showering that wakes you up, then, but a regular, mechanical thump. Makes you think of aliens. If there are cow mutilations, will the evangelicals come looking for you?

If they find out you're a certified witch, it might be the end of your whole family. And you'd feel bad for the animals.

The noise is a tractor and baler. It's hot-cold — you can't decide how you feel in the dry air at one-thirty in the morning — and still, so the sound carries. Round and round in the dark, baling up the cut grass and pushing it out in little rectangular turds. Every so often, one falls apart while you watch.

Light flares from the tractor. It's an old one, you think. No cab on it. It might be blue. It's carrying a redneck.

He's pretty. Not the way you liked boys when you lived here before. You liked femme creatures, then. You cut out pictures of The Coreys from magazines Bernie shoplifted for you. No body hair, big eyes. Boys who looked like baby dykes.

You didn't expect to enjoy it when the boys you knew turned into guys, and then, all at once, into men. They got thick in the chest and their necks disappeared. Hairier and suddenly balding. But that's when you started to like men for real. Maybe you'd been waiting for them to transform, and then some hormonal switch in you flipped and you understood what May'd meant when she said she liked hairy men to keep her warm.

The back isn't hairy on this one. He's driving without a shirt, and while you can't see much, there's a distinct boundary between the light of him and the dark. Big round farmer shoulders. You didn't know you liked that.

So you wait until he circles around. The next time his lights sweep across the fence, you wave.

He pauses, like he thinks what he sees is just an animal. Then stands up and peers.

"Hello?"

"Hey," you say.

He looks harder. "Jesus. Amory?"

"Hey."

It's your landlord.

Ryan's older than you. You remember that because he sat behind you on the school bus. One of your friends had a crush on him. She was older than you, and he was older than her, and she made this big show out of wanting his phone number. Your mom caught wind of that. Told Ryan your friend wanted to talk to him.

Your friend melted right down when he asked her what the hell she wanted to talk to him about. Never got a word of an explanation past her lips. She didn't come over after that. Said she liked you fine but she was finished with your mom.

Your mom forgot you were just a kid, but she forgot she was an adult, too.

And maybe it's hormones, or you think you've wandered into porn, because the night feeds that sort of thing. Because you grin and say, "You look good."

He does, though maybe he doesn't think so. He's easily fifty pounds heavier than the last time you saw him. He has half a beard.

"What? Oh. Um, thanks." Then this half-look like he thinks you might be making fun of him, like he's forgotten which side of that mockery he was always on. "What's up? Is your mom okay?"

"She's fine. I wanted some air. I thought you might be aliens."

"Nope. Just haying."

You look at him. He used to be such a flirt, you think. He got old while you were fucking around. He should come over. You say, "You should come over." It comes right out of your mouth, like you're possessed by the spirit of your mom.

"Seriously, is something wrong?"

"No. Just, come over. I'll make you breakfast."

4.

The years you spent as a vegan were the same ones you spent as a smoker, and you're not sure they're not related. Like, maybe you couldn't taste things anyway, so it didn't matter if the food was awful. You're lapsed, now. A sometime vegetarian, mostly because you feel bad for the animals. The urge to free the cows next door — Ryan's cows, you guess — is only off-set by the cheap rent on the house, and your apparent interest in his grown-up ass.

If you weren't so focused on the animals, you'd have a job now. There's a new, giant industrial hog barn less than half a mile away. It stinks every time the prevailing wind shifts. They're always looking to hire people. It's a sterile environment, and hard work, but they hire locals as part of a goodwill policy, and you're pretty sure they'd hire you. Better than minimum wage. It'd be a short commute.

Something to think about while you cook the bacon.

You couldn't really work there. You've protested industrial hog farming. If you had to actually look at the sow stalls, at the pain of the animals, you wouldn't be able to cope. You'd have to start making calls up the family phone tree until you found Bernie's eco-terrorists, and call in a strike.

Free the swine!

The bacon smells amazing. It's why you lapsed, the first time. And there was some in the basement deep-freeze when you looked today. You're not sure how old it is, but the freezer burn isn't bad, and cooked up the meat smells good. You're off the hook because you didn't buy it. Like fur, you think. You didn't want the animal killed, but now that it's dead, you shouldn't waste it, and cheapen its sacrifice.

Ryan doesn't come before the bacon's cold. You eat slices of it with your fingers, then carry the rest upstairs on a paper towel for your mom. She isn't, strictly speaking, awake. The smell works on her, though. She rouses, and reaches out of her blanket-pile for food.

"Do you remember I used to feed you in the middle of the night?" she asks.

You think about that. "I don't think it was the middle of the night." You're not sure, though. You remember her getting you out of bed and settling you next to her on the couch to eat brownies. Your father was there, sometimes. Not usually your sisters, even when they lived at home. Or she'd bring you handfuls of snacks from parties they were having downstairs.

Her and your father. Your sisters' parties were out in the woods, the way yours would have been, later, if you'd stayed. But your mom and your father used to have parties. They'd have friends over — old hippies, maturing into civil servants and lawyers — and stay up hours after she'd packed you in. And then, while you were drifting, she'd come in, her hands full of salty snacks and the odd potluck contributions her friends had brought.

Slippery potstickers. Curried rice noodles. The first sushi of your life.

Wasabi on your five-year-old tongue.

You say, "I've been disappointed by a man. Eat his bacon and go back to sleep."

She fully opens her eyes and looks at you. "Anyone I know?"

"No."

"Ryan, then," she says.

You shrug.

"I know Ryan. Sweet man. He's good at disappointing women, though. Remember when he disappointed your friend? Annie?"

"I don't think it counted as a disappointment."

"She was disappointed." Your mother curls back into herself. "God I'm tired these days."

It's not a surprise: she's been exhausted for years. You remember before she retired, she'd spend whole weekends in bed. If you came over, if you warned her first, she'd make out she was reading, and bed was where she liked to read. If you just let yourself in, she might not even wake up. You'd dig through her shelves to see if there was anything worth reading, and maybe borrow money. Leave her a note about the books.

When you took off for Ontario, you thought at least she wouldn't get into trouble. Her earlier slutty phase was more alarming. She found men on the Internet. That was maybe circa 2002. The men weren't dangerous — the mythology of the internet aside, you don't think a lot of oversharing middle-aged sluts actually do get murdered by internet people — but you'd have given a lot for her slutty phase not to coincide with yours.

Your father's slutty phase you manage not to think about.

You don't think you picked it up from her. Maybe from your sisters, or one of the covens that turned out to be more free-love-oriented than you expected. But you enjoyed your slutty phase pretty thoroughly. You didn't think you'd lost the knack of propositioning.

It might be just that you're living with your mother. Or that Ryan knows you, has known you for years. Just because you can see him as an adult doesn't mean that he can see you.

5.

You picked up the running habit in Winnipeg, when you could go run the long blocks full of original-owner bungalows in River Heights and nobody would come out to chase you. Not even to walk a dog. Widows lived in those houses. They stayed up late watching TV with their sheers open, so you could see them. Lady after lady in her coffee-toned Wonderbra, drinking a mug of whatever and flipping channels.

You particularly remember this one lady who'd sit there with nothing on top at all, but that wasn't nearly as interesting as the parrot roosting on her head.

She fed it popcorn out of the bowl in her lap. They looked happy enough. One time she stood up — maybe to answer the phone? — and you learned she was wearing green elastic-waist pants a shade or two darker than the parrot.

You weren't running so much as standing there watching, camouflaged as a woman trying to gasp her lungs back into her body, too breathless to look in people's windows. Not looking at the obvious.

You keep running. Follow the deer trails through the pasture for a while, while the full moon's bright enough for you to see. After the phase shifts to crescent, though, you need to find your way better, or at least be surer of your footing. Once your eyes adjust, you can see the road even by starlight. So you go back to that. And then you shift to early mornings, but when you go back into the trees, you disturb the deer.

Just a bit, you wonder if your mom would look for you, if you fell. If she'd just assume you took off back to wherever you came to visit her from. They'd find your skeleton in the sand and leaf-loam in a decade, just bones left, and she'd tell the cops it couldn't be you, because you were in Calgary and just not phoning much, and anyway, the second tiny set of bones couldn't possibly be yours. You'd have mentioned that to her, at some point.

If it has bones already. You aren't sure.

You run along the road. If you time it just right, no cars come by at all.

There's a TV ad you remember, where a woman stands in a field of bizarre flags, and she wonders where she is, because she never ran this far before. You don't have that kind of range, but you cut through someone else's pasture — open ground, no bush, so the deer can see you coming — and stagger across a farmstead you actually don't remember, and the feeling is the same.

It's minimalist. There's a trailer in the yard, and a bunch of cattle pens back behind it. Decaying round hay bales provide some shelter. It looks like a dozen farmyards you remember;

you just didn't think there was one *here*. But then you scramble up the end of the bale row, to get your bearings from higher ground, and it snaps into place. The original house is gone, but its foundation is still visible, and uncharred. They might only have moved the building. The trailer's new. And you remember facing some kind of person, up on the bales, while you were down below, in a car.

One of Bernie's friends, you think it was. Older than you. You came here with her, to get something, or do something, because your mom left Bernie in charge of you for the day. Your sisters were terrible babysitters. They kept including you, like you were old enough to keep up with them.

You're still sitting on the bale-stack, cross-legged now, when he comes out of the trailer. Cellphone guy. He cocks his head, trying to make you out in the early daylight. Then he shrugs, like if you're not setting fires, you're not a problem. You can sit there all day and catch mice. He throws a bag in the truck and goes to leave.

You say, "How's your wife?"

"I'm not married."

"How's —"

"I'm not. I promise."

You're not sure why he backed off, then. He looks so much like a dedicated Christian: a little too into being the man of the house, so deeply devoted to outreach that he'll reach out to the battered dykey witches of the district. Men like that always have an edge of proposition. You remember May complaining that the combination of sleaze and holiness hurt her sinuses, like too much sugar. Too damn *nice. Don't trust a man who won't tell you what he wants until after you've got your panties off,* your mom said. *He won't give you a decent answer any time you're not naked.*

He studies you. Open like a missionary waiting for the moment of conversion. "Ryan said you offered to make him breakfast."

"I did."

"He thought it might not be appropriate."

"Oh God."

"Because he's your landlord. He thought you might be. Well."

You think about this. "Trying to fuck him for a break on the rent? Oh god, I'm not that desperate yet."

He cocks his head at you. "Will you make me breakfast?"

"I don't owe you rent."

He sighs. "I just. Ryan suggested I should ask you. I work at the pig barn, you know? And sometimes I don't feel up to cooking. I thought maybe you could make me breakfast. Or lunch, or something."

You try to give him the flat stare that Bernie taught you to make men in bars go away.

"I mean, I'd pay you, for hot meals sometimes."

"I'll think about it."

"Can I stop by?"

You answer him. Make sure your tone says *don't do me any favours*.

6.

You only cooked professionally one summer (fall, early winter), when May's roommate asked you to come up north with him. He kept talking about this homestead colony that his friend grew up in, up on the border between the Yukon and British Columbia. His parents had gone up there in the 60s after reading *Steal This Book*, to be the new frontier people. Built cabins and gardens, and then cooler things like a bathhouse and an outdoor hot tub they heated with wood fires. It sounded amazing. He might have made it up, though, because once you got to Dawson Creek, he changed his mind, and you both wound up in a logging camp.

You tried logging for a couple of days. You weren't the only girl up there, but you were the only one who could dislocate her shoulder just by pulling too hard on a chain.

After the medic set your shoulder and gave you a handful of dusty, maybe-expired painkillers, you wandered up to the kitchens. Most of the cooking was done by just one woman. Lorna. She had a daughter with some kind of psych problems who lived in supported housing in Edmonton, and Lorna said it was easier for her to be out of town a lot of the time. It meant they fought less. She spent about half the year cooking in logging camps, and the other half on EI or welfare, reading library books.

Cooking for loggers was basic. You produced a lot of red meat dishes, and baked a lot of bread. Basic kinds of veggies to ward off scurvy. You fried a lot of eggs and learned to make better coffee.

It's maybe the best skill you have. Your mom's opinions on your bone structure aside, what you mostly share with your sisters is a willingness to blow off a shit job and try a new place. Your mom's office career kept tying her to jobs she didn't like. It ground her down. If she'd been a better cook and a worse bookkeeper, she might not be early-retired and living on the edge of financial collapse in a house that she used to own and now rents from a neighbour.

You could always hook, if you need to, your mom said. To May and Bernie, and then to you while you were still fairly little. To make ends meet. Men like big girls. You might be able to build up a real clientele.

You didn't try it. But you've cooked breakfast for a fair number of strange men, one way or another.

You're medium-sure you cooked breakfast for the last guy, the one who got you pregnant. He was a sweetheart. You met him at an after-party in Winnipeg. The kind of thing you blame your upbringing for. Winnipeg has this amazing fetish scene. You were never all that kinky — making sex formal and pre-planned never worked for you — but you liked the company. The bimonthly organized parties in Osborne Village were half dungeon and half dance club. You went with friends the first time, for kicks, but the room had good energy. Everyone was friendly, and careful, and there were rules about who could and couldn't touch you. If anyone got closer than you wanted, big guys in expensive latex dragged him away, threw him out in the street, and made it clear that if he came back, it wouldn't be kinky fun. They'd call the cops.

No touching girls without their permission. No touching *anyone*.

With permission, though —

You spent time just cuddled up at the edge of the dance floor with people you only half-knew, who were feeling too quiet for dancing or impact-play. Boys — men, but really boys, like the ones you remember from high school — braided your hair into actual cornrows, and this gorgeous woman told your fortune. She was beyond pregnant. Heavy like gravity had come for her. Probably due any minute, but she was drinking bottled water and swaying to the honestly-really-bad-but-whatever music like she wasn't carrying fifty extra pounds and a tiny human visibly kicking at her belly from the inside.

You doubt you'll be that graceful about it. Even if you hit the thrift stores for old broomstick skirts you can just sling down below your belly, you aren't likely to develop that intense femininity, or the style to carry it off.

Not that you can't do feminine. It's just that you do it best when you're naked. Women's clothes don't really work on your body, and guys' clothes aren't quite the right length for any part of you. But stripped down, you have the breasts and hips of the mythological warrior your mom likes to imagine you as. Two breasts, and you're no archer, but still.

You could start walking around the house naked. Your mom wouldn't notice. Or she'd just make an approving noise and go back to bed. Or she might join you.

He comes to the door, though, and you're hit with a moment of wild propriety. You don't have a bra on, or socks. You can smell yourself. You'd run, but he offered you money; you have to let him in.

It's early for him. You haven't been to bed yet. You thought if you shifted onto your mom's schedule, she might talk to you. Come down and protect you from strangers, to make up for the years that she didn't. She still might do it. You just haven't explained to her that it's what you want.

"It's oatmeal," you say.

He's disappointed. You're pretty sure he was thinking of diner-quality breakfast. But he takes his boots off carefully and leaves them on the mat, and comes to sit at the table. Hat off, hands folded in his lap. Looks at you hopefully.

So you give him oatmeal. It's basic, but you ate it for the first month, when you felt sick all the time. The way you learned to eat it in Winnipeg, at the Amy's Cafe branch where you worked for a bit. Oatmeal first, then throw on butter and handfuls of brown sugar. The result's more like a cookie than anything healthy, but it's a completely different experience than the grey slime with milk that you grew up with, and no part of it's been microwaved. No synthetic apple-cinnamon flavours.

You eat standing up and watch him.

He looks up at you a couple of times. Smiles a bit. Finishes everything, drinks the orange juice you provided in a plastic cup, and stands. Asks, "What do I owe you?"

"I don't know. Three bucks."

He digs in his pocket and comes out with the handful of change guys always seem to have. Counts out three loonies, and then two extra quarters.

"Tip."

"Thanks."

"Say hi to your mom for me?"

He leaves, putting his hat back on once he's outside, and it occurs to you that it's going to be a real problem how you don't know his name. He knows who you are, and details about your life, like the sexual paranoia of your busmate-cum-landlord, and maybe a bit about the state of your mom. You're past the point you could ask him.

He's asked if you could cook him breakfast again tomorrow.

It's not a good reason to go dig around in his house, but you don't have a better idea. He locks his door, at least. When you were a kid, you don't remember anybody locking their doors. Your family never did. Your mom said it was because if somebody needed to get in to use the phone or something, they should be able to. And you didn't really have anything worth stealing.

It wasn't quite true then. It might be true now.

He locks his door and keeps the keys on a nail under the built-up porch, right by the steps.

7.

So you got pregnant. As far as you can tell, from counting, it was after the after-party, after the fetish party in April. You hung out on a crappy, low-slung couch in a pile of afghans that rivalled your mom's. Got companionably high.

This guy you'd made out with a couple of times before was there, sort of leaning on your leg. He ran his fingers along your shin. Stopped when he hit the jagged area of your shin splints and then carefully outlined the bone shards. "Does it hurt?"

"Only if I run on it."

"Can I touch?"

"You are touching. Sure. Yes. You can touch."

He kissed your stubbly legs. Ran his hand up to the line of your panties, where the hair was creeping out, and what happened to your pants? You think maybe you didn't wear any to the party. They're those kinds of parties — there's practically a no-pants rule, as much as there can be in a licensed bar, where actual nakedness would probably bring health inspectors, or at least cops. So you probably just wore a long coat and runners. Like a flasher.

He went down on you. He wasn't amazing, but it was sweet. And you wanted to fuck him, so you took him home.

Both of you were half-stoned and exhausted. You had friendly, gropy sex, and then you made him breakfast and gave him a kiss before he took off for work. Said he had an afternoon Sunday shift. Fair enough.

He scribbled his first name and an e-mail on your shopping list, and you grinned at it and threw it away. Figured you'd see him at the next party.

Instead you moved home to live with your hibernating mom and break into the neighbour's trailer while he's at work.

His place is full of stuff — some of it newish, from Walmart, the rest of it salvaged or retrieved from somewhere like the Mennonite secondhand furniture place. Old couch, old table with blue formica, too chipped and messed up to qualify as vintage. There's a bagful of clothes on the floor of his bedroom next to a single bed on a frame with the tacky remains of stickers still lurking on the headboard.

His bathroom's full of pills. You don't recognize most of them, but short of full-on psychosis, you can't think of anything mental that would require this tangle.

In a drawer in the kitchen, you find old plastic wallet-size cards held together with a rubber band. Some of them are discount memberships for supermarkets, or points-collectors for different kinds of intensely normal businesses. Others are government cards, so cracked and broken that you cut your finger on a shard. Old school IDs.

If they represent his taste in girls, though, you know why he likes you. The girl on the card looks back at you with a kid-face that's not yours, but could have been, if you'd stayed out in this backwater and never discovered eyeliner. The card's old enough to *be* one of yours.

One of those token things high school kids do. Girls get guys' sports jackets. Guys get girls' expired student cards.

She looks like you. Like every girl you were ever friends with. And maybe you were friends with her.

You were. You remember.

You remember Crystal Wilcox the way you remember people you used to be friends with in the period before you became yourself. The end of that period changes as you get older. For a long time, it ended when your family moved to Saskatoon. Later, it ended when high school ended. Right now, it ends sometime in your early twenties, about the time you would have finished university if you'd finished university. When you first moved to Calgary and re-formed yourself in a new pool of friends. Your furnished basement bachelor only had as much of your "before" things as you'd carried in your backpack and your pockets. Like a gift: new clothes, new books, new stuff. New girl. So much it got to be a habit. Every three or four years, you get rid of the old version of yourself and start over.

You burned the old stuff once. It was a shitty building, and if you hadn't been burning things in the sink, something else or someone else would still have sent it up. Cigarettes or one of the old space heaters, or a stove left on when people were finished doing hot knives.

No one said *arson*, and you got new stuff and moved to a new town.

Crystal.

Crystal was this girl you were sort of friends with. She rode the school bus, you think. Sat ahead of you. You were in the same grade, or maybe just the same class in a split-grade class-room. The year you were in the portable classroom out behind the elementary school. She was your partner for some kind of small project.

Yes. She was a year older than you, but not good at making friends her own age, so you were going to be her friend. She came up with this elaborate story that you and she acted out at recess, in one of the old structures on the playground.

It was okay. It was fun.

You can almost picture her. She comes back easier than the interior of the apartment that burned down.

Your mom said, *Screw insurance. Just try not to own anything that costs more than fifteen dollars.*

"That's a redneck joke."

"It applies."

"We're not rednecks."

"You're not. I'll be whatever I want to. You can be a hipster arsonist if it makes you happy."

She has no idea. Or she might. You remember her catching

you with Bernie's matches, when you were little, and making the point that you should keep your fires contained, and not in the house.

Not in the house is the rule for practically everything.

You keep Crystal's student card. She feels like company.

While you're walking home, favouring your left shin, you wonder if she's buried in his basement. In the basement of the gone-now house, since the trailer almost certainly doesn't have a basement of its own. He keeps looking at you in this warm, friendly way, like he's come courting. And you broke into his house. It would be very Bluebeard-y.

The storyteller who came to your school when you were kids told that story, Bluebeard, in the library, and you were sitting next to Crystal. But she wasn't very smart: it would figure that she didn't take the warning.

Your mom's asleep, and she doesn't wake up when you come into her room. Even while the ancient modem's screaming along the phone lines, she only growls at you and curls deeper into her bed.

It's the best idea you have: run a Facebook search for Crystal Wilcox. Only, there's no Crystal Wilcox listed in your region. There are girls and women in other cities and other countries, but they're all the wrong age or the wrong race or they belong to improbable evangelical groups. So you look up the Swanson Elementary School alumni group. If you can be an alumnus of anything, there's a group for it. We all graduated from kindergarten! Who remembers that time we all went to the park and got sunburned? Clean, friendly stuff without much acrimony.

Your mom groans in her sleep. You get up and go to the bathroom and come back, and the page is still loading. Slow, slow internet, coming in over ancient phone lines that keep being struck by lightning or snapping in the cold.

You forget, sometimes, that the Internet exists. Coming here has been too much like going back in time. If you stay much longer, you'll turn back into your kid-self, and in a few months you'll be a little girl holding a baby like a doll. You'll stare at it like you stared at dolls, and then just leave it in a room and go do something else.

This isn't good for you.

Swanson Elementary Alumni page. Half the kids listed you don't know. More than half. They're kids who've gone to school since you stopped living out here. Some of them are young enough to be your kids.

There's no Crystal Wilcox. There is a Chris Wilcox. And there he is, easier to identify online than by anything in his house.

Click to go to his profile. It tells you nothing much. There's a picture of him, grinning, with a snow-and-bare-trees back-drop. Selfie shot, but decently well-done. Everything else is friends-locked.

Your mom stretches out so that her foot presses into the small of your back. Her afghans pool on the floor, under your ass. The computer fan groans and your mom shifts again. For a second, you think she's kicked you hard enough to push right through your spine.

8.

May calls to talk to your mom. You say, "She's sleeping."

"It's four in the afternoon."

"Yeah. I know."

"Is she okay?"

"She went out on disability and then took early retirement. She hasn't been okay for years."

For a second you think May's going to argue with you. May's spent her life being the one who talks shit about your

202 • YOU ARE NOT NEEDED NOW

mom, so she gets her hackles up if you suggest anything about your mom is less than perfect.

"Is she worse than usual?"

You say, "I'm pregnant."

Pause. "How far along?"

"Five months."

"How's mom?"

"She hasn't noticed." You really don't think she has. It's not a good sign. Your mom's always been able to tell what was going on inside your skin. She can be a bit explicit about the whole thing. When you were a teenager, you wondered out loud once how she timed asking if you needed more tampons, and she said she could smell you.

"It's nothing to worry about. I can smell all of you. And me. It's just something I'm attuned to. I can smell the ladies at work, too."

She's been able to detect bad moods and skin rashes and your first yeast infection. You let May think about that.

She says, "Boy or girl?"

"I don't know."

"Going for the surprise?"

"I haven't checked."

May huffs at you. "Amory, and I say this as the mother of three accidental children, get your ass to the doctor."

"I'm not *sick*."

"You need blood tests."

"Women have been having babies for centuries."

"Alone in the woods with their crazy mothers?"

"Especially there." You settle against the counter. The phone's left over from the last time you lived in the house: it's yellowish moulded plastic with a long, tangled cord. Low-tech in a way you find vaguely unsettling, like you've fallen back in time and you really are eleven years old. And a pregnant witch in the woods. "I'm running. I'm doing yoga. I'm eating real food. One of the neighbourhood guys started paying me to cook him breakfast."

"Anybody I know?"

"You know Chris Wilcox?"

May thinks. You can hear her. "No. But that doesn't mean anything. If he's your age, I wouldn't ever have noticed him."

"He lives down the end of the road. Where Bernie's dealer used to live."

"Sorry, that doesn't help. I had my own dealer."

You hang up on her. Walk outside. It's hot, but drier than Winnipeg. You don't melt so much as gradually dissolve. In the trees, it's cool enough for you to move freely. You've been thinking about sleeping outside. It's hot even at night, and you could bed down in the open air. Dig yourself a pit and build the framework of a shrine like you learned at camp. Worship your own body until you can put that second heartbeat into sync with your primary one.

You peel your clothes off. Insects fall onto your skin, swim in the sweat-pool in the small of your back. It's cooler once you're naked. Your navel popped, sometime in the last day or two, and your belly's now aggressively convex. Your scalp itches.

You walk naked back to the house and dig around in the bathroom until you come up with a handful of ancient, tiny elastics. Beads and buttons in a jar from some old art project. One of your mom's tie-dyed tablecloths. A handful of magazines and books.

Living outside has its moments. You separate your hair into sections and braid each one. It's not long enough to be elegant, and you haven't done this often enough to be able to achieve full cornrows, but you can put it up out of your face. If you start working on it now, you might be able to re-establish the dreadlocks you had for a while when you were up north.

The thing inside you kicks. If it comes out as shaggy as you did, you'll be able to work its scalp into a tiny version of your mess. Live together as tree people.

Your mom comes downstairs, eventually, in the evening. You can see light, faintly, in the window. You wait. Stretch out in the brome grass. There are ants on your legs. She comes out into the yard.

She hasn't been outside in fifteen days. You've been keeping count. She goes into Saskatoon maybe once a month, to file things, and comes back exhausted, so that she sleeps downstairs, not even crawling back to her room. Her eyes are narrowed in the too-bright evening. Looking for you.

You wait. She wanders over. Says, "I was going to have a glass of wine. Did you want one?"

You say, "I'm pregnant."

It's like her not to comment on your nakedness. You have a vague sense she's pleased you haven't started shaving your legs again, but the impression is only a sideways flick of her lashes. She says, "I must be congested, not to have noticed."

You shrug.

She brings you out lemonade in a sealer jar, and a can of bug spray. "Do you want a sleeping bag?"

"I like the grass."

"Enjoy your communion, then."

It does get dark, eventually. Nine-twenty at night. The stars are thick. You can see the residual Milky Way light, now that the house lights are dimmed to the monitor's glow. If you went in now, the phone would scream at you. Outside, there are only bugs singing.

9.

May comes down from Meadow Lake by car and brings you vitamins and an overflowing back seat stuffed with the mess of a secondhand store. Baby things. It's everything her kids have outgrown. Her youngest is three now, and you'd kind of assumed she was looking to get pregnant again.

"I'm having my tubes tied," she announces. "On the drive home."

"They offer roadside snips?"

"I'm crashing with a friend in the city."

"Kids okay without you?"

"They're with their dads. They'll survive."

She carries the tied-off grocery bags into the house four at a time, looping back around you for the next load. They pile up in the kitchen like accidental charity. Bag after unwanted bag. She staggers past you with an armful of flat-packed furniture held into a single mass with crinkly brown packing tape.

"I am done," she says, though she's not done. The next load's plastic: a tiny bathtub, a booster seat, a bundle of small dishes wrapped with clear packing tape. She's brought you a baggie of soothers and teething toys. Most of them are covered with lint. "You'll have to clean those. Just boil them. I threw away the ones that weren't still good."

The bassinet, when she brings it, is full of stuffed animals. "These are new, more or less."

You say, "Don't buy me stuff."

"I'm buying you groceries before I go, but I didn't pay for any of this lot. Do you remember stuffed animals?"

"These ones?"

"Yours. The ones we had when we were kids."

"Sure." You had a set of them. A brown bunny, a bear wearing 1978 Commonwealth Games overalls (handed down from Bernie), a music box bear that you wound until its tiny internal gears snapped, a battered unicorn that was May's home economics project in grade eight, six knitted mice, a hard-stuffed kangaroo, your giant christening-gift frog, the velvet dog your mom sewed you for Christmas because you wanted a brand-name Pound Puppy™, and a Raggedy Ann. You think there might have been a sock monkey and an old Cabbage Patch Kid.

It occurs to you that the frog was tangible evidence your parents were at one point at least nominally Christian. There might even have been a rosary or something, to go with the frog, though if it had still lurked among your possessions by your pre-teens, you'd have taken it apart to use as vampire repellant.

May says, "Well, stuffed animals are cheap now. Really cheap. Softer than our best ones and you can buy them for eight bucks at gas stations. They invade the house every time I get pregnant. It's a fucking zoo."

The giraffe she levers out of the back passenger-side footwell is, fully extended, almost as big as you are. She pushes the thing into your arms. "Would you believe this is the *second* giraffe?"

It smells like factory chemicals and arrowroot cookies. You hold its spotted neck against your swelling body. You say, "Your name is Max."

"I'm glad you're willing to name *something*. Anyhow. Get ready for an annual stuffie purge. Have a bonfire or something. Don't tell your friends. Nobody just drops by with a bunch of receiving blankets." She hands you another bag. "Receiving blankets. They come from Walmart."

"I don't shop at Walmart."

"You do now."

Her car is a clown car. Its muted Cavalier blue conceals an infinite interior, still spewing forth baby supplies. Most of them are textiles. May narrates. She's furious about the stuffed animals. Too many. They fuck in the closets and produce new, silky-soft Easter bunnies clutching felt carrots or flowers.

May has five kids under eleven and a full-Jungian aura of maternal competence that fools people into thinking she's a nice person. She looks good because her friends haven't met the rest of you, and so they don't know what she's really like. You wonder if she's been thinking about burning the children, or just their soft-toy possessions.

It's easy. You just bathe them in camping fuel and strike a spark.

"Amory?"

"I'm going to go lie down."

Outside. You've dug yourself a hollow in the trees, lined it with grass. You keep the tablecloth folded in a tree-crook, so it's handy if you want to spread it out in the branches for shade.

Sometime in the last week, your hollow grew a Rubbermaid storage tub holding juice boxes and store-brand cookies. It has to be from Chris, or Ryan. Your mom wouldn't empty, clean, and seal a box just for this. And sometimes you catch glimpses of Ryan. He walks the barbed-wire fence line, checking it for ruptures like he thinks the hayfield might burst out and overrun your yard. Force him to come tearing after it with a scythe.

You're hopeful even in your stretched-out skin. The friendly, almost-morning fuck that warped your body was the last time you got laid. That one was pretty, and you suppose, biologically speaking, that he did the job, but you want something a bit more

208 · YOU ARE NOT NEEDED NOW

male-bodied. Even at twenty yards' cautious distance, Ryan smells like salty-ocean deodorant and agricultural pheromones. If he takes one step past the fence line, you're going to climb him like a tree.

So it's not surprising, really, that he watches you like some medieval villager afeared of a witch. You're getting stranger the longer you spend cooped up with your mom. Enough you've started doing outdoor naked yoga just like your too-firm bulging gut isn't a thing.

He saw you. You're almost sure.

He keeps coming back.

Later — just a few months, now — you can mark out his front door in menstrual blood and watch him lose his mind. If he asks, you'll tell him it's just deer blood from roadkill. He'll think that's better. You can't imagine why Ryan would be happier with the idea of you sticking your fingers into dead animals than your own body, but he might never recover if he finds out the blood is yours. That it's cunt-blood. Still, he'll smell you. He'll be attuned to it, the next time you approach him. Ask him out to coffee in the daylight, like a sane woman.

You can only hope he doesn't go to a church that'll burn you on sight.

May brings you a glass of water and touches your head. She says, "What did you do to your hair?"

"It was bothering me."

"You did a shit job if you were trying to get to a no-wash point. Let me redo it. If you go in looking like that, not only will they not give you welfare, they'll probably send you in for psych review."

"I can pass one."

"As long as you don't mention the arsonist tendencies."

"Who told you? Mom?"

"Bernie."

Bernie used to burn things in the fire pit behind the house. She taught you about controlled sparks.

She'd steal things from girls in her class if they bothered her. You've always been weird, all of you, but Bernie attracted hostility on a different level. Her storage shelves at school were vandalized. Her pencil boxes were stolen weekly until she found a canvas surplus bag and transformed it into the basket-case purse of doom. Filled it with pens, tampons, sugar packets from restaurants, cigarettes, twists of toilet paper to help start fires. Bernie had an eye for the things that people really liked and still wouldn't miss right away: magazines, lip gloss, hair elastics, folded passed notes.

Bernie, you recall, taught you to do hot knives, too, when she was supposed to be babysitting.

You say, "I don't need welfare. I'll get a job."

"Where?"

"The pig barn."

"You won't. Pig shit is toxic to fetal development. It's bad enough you smoke."

"I quit."

"Good girl. I'll take you in to apply. I know what to tell them. You just look humble, and try not to set anyone on fire."

She hauls you indoors and levers you into the shallow, retro-avocado bathtub. Leaves and mud fall when she pours water over your head. May tugs at the mats, undoes them, and rubs cheap conditioner into your scalp. "You look good," she says.

"I've been running."

"Yeah?" Water falls from the plastic juice pitcher over your shoulders.

"I can do 3k when it's not so hot. I have decent shoes, even. I got fitted for them at this running store in Winnipeg. They said my feet roll to the inside."

"So do mine. It's why we walk that way."

She clears a space in the living-room, sits you on a flattened bed-pillow and starts sectioning your hair. You're expecting the pull of rubber bands, but she uses something softer. It's an elastic, but you can feel twists of something like plastic excelsior fuzzing away from the core.

May backcombs each section into dreadlocks, inch by inch. Your hair's short for the process, really, but you can feel her working you into a consistent shape. Tufts all over your head start to twist in on themselves.

It's the most intimate contact you've had with another human being in five and a half months. May works your scalp as well as your hair, rubbing in what might be beeswax or hand lotion to help it tangle. You sit still enough in the house's half-dark that you start to shiver, and she makes you go get dressed.

"Sorry I'm edgy."

"It's fine. Normal for — what is it, month five?"

"Six."

"Mmm. Headed for the third trimester. How are the hormones?"

"I thought about cursing Ryan's house and sleep because he won't fuck me."

"Neighbour Ryan?"

"He's our landlord, too."

"You should do it. If you're good enough in the sack, he might give you a break on the rent. Have you seen Mom's bank account?"

"No."

"Well. Consider whoring yourself out. It's not like you can get any more pregnant."

"He's not obliging."

"He's scared of you. It's your own fault for telling all those school bus kids you were a witch."

"I did that," you think about it, "twenty-three years ago."

"I bet they still remember. Still, it's good to be feared." She tugs on your hair. "Just keep it under control while we're talking to the government."

10.

You go on welfare. You need the money. May goes through the fridge, sees what's in it, and mutters about the need for food stamps and how you could at least have started a garden, so you could be weird instead of just poor.

In the city, May buys you bags of vegan-smoothie ingredients before she puts you back where she found you.

Chris is in the kitchen, doing your dishes.

He took his boots off at the door. They're clean, actually. You remember May telling you that the pig barn workers have to be fully sterile. He works in there in a white, crinkly suit like a mattress cover.

You push the food into the fridge. Load in the wine for your mom, because really, it's the least you could bring her. You think May might have paid for that, too, though. You haven't checked to see if she folded a couple of twenties into the groceries. Chris' food is there, too. He's brought bacon, and pork sausages.

"Did you make these yourself?"

"We don't process at work, you know. Just feed and clean up some."

May cocks her head. You keep expecting Chris to turn his

head towards her: May's hard to ignore. She has all your mom's personal force, and she's amazonian-tall. More so even than the rest of you — evidence of the other-dad she has, and that you don't talk about. "Crystal?"

"It's just Chris. For a while now."

"Sorry. Bad manners. But I was trying to place you."

"If I tell you you're right," he says, "will you drop it?"

"Yeah. Sorry."

He shrugs. You stare into the fridge and try to decide why you thought him murdering Crystal was more plausible than him being her.

"I made myself breakfast. You weren't here."

You straighten. If he's been supplying your snack-box, he's seen you naked, but he hasn't seen you in May's maternity clothes before. They have the same problem all her hand-me-downs do, namely that she's six inches taller than you are. The skirt that probably skimmed her calves brushes your feet. But it might look better on you. It isn't really maternity-wear, but the elastic waist lets it sling under your belly.

Chris says, "It's okay, May. You should go say hi to your mom, if you're leaving. She seems a bit..."

You say, "Yeah."

May shakes her head. She clamps a hand around your wrist for a second, then lets go and leaves. In her absence, you can feel your bones spark.

Your job now. Childbearing. Mother control.

You say, "I'll do the dishes. Get out."

In one of May's bags, you find a seamless band of jersey-knit fabric that you think at first is a tube top but turns out to be a belly-wrap. It holds you tight enough that you can keep running. Your shoes hold up to the gravel roads, and the bush trails, and your range has increased enough that you can watch the neighbours. You aren't the only one who's awake half the night. No one in the country covers their windows, and they aren't looking for you, looking at them.

The old people who live south of Ryan go to bed early, but the man wakes up at night and comes outside to pee. He wears jockey shorts and boots. Smokes while he's outside and then stubs the butts into a can under the porch.

Farther down the road, there's a house you don't remember, and the yard is full of animals. Goats and a donkey. Pigs that sleep tucked up against the house. Chickens in the trees. Almost but not quite your people. The animal traces don't offset the cross on their door and the doormat praising Jesus. You walk softly until you realize there's no dog, and the pigs don't mind you.

The goose is a shock. It doesn't even scream first, just bites down on your thigh.

You've never fought a bird before. Its wings are huge, and you're forced to retreat without finding out what they keep in the barn.

Your leg bruises almost black. There's raw blood just under the surface of your skin.

It slows you down. You can't stay home, but it hurts like a bitch. If you weren't sure you could walk, you'd think the bird had broken your leg.

Add it to the list of future curses — something for the evangelical zoo.

You're tempted to put together something that meets all the satanic criteria you remember from childhood, just to see if you can convince them that the rumoured cults of the eighties and nineties have returned to haunt rural Saskatchewan.

It's an idea.

You're limping more than running when you unlock Chris' door and wake him up.

You say, "I want to curse someone."

Chris stares at you. He's shirtless in bed, and you can see the scars under his pecs from what must have been pretty radical surgery, but it's less noticeable than his chest hair and the beard you didn't fully register before.

"Your neighbours' bird attacked me."

"Why are you in my bedroom?"

"You let yourself into *my* house."

He shakes his head. "I never crawled into bed with you."

"Not yet, anyway. You're not Christian, are you?"

Chris pushes himself up. Gets out of bed and goes looking for pants.

He doesn't look like he was ever Crystal, except for the absence you can only half-see before he turns away from you. He looks fundamentally male in ways you weren't expecting, and there's nothing girly in his body. You're surprised, really, that he didn't set you off when your pregnancy-lust first kicked in. With his jeans on, commando over his hips, he looks even more fundamentally like your type.

He smells off, you think. Or something.

"My faith is not your business. Do you want something to eat?"

"I ate already. I just. I don't like having them there, so close by."

"They don't much like you either, but they haven't commissioned a tribunal or summoned the Inquisition. Let them be."

"Their goose bit me."

"Stop crawling around their yard, then." He steps closer. "Amory, I'm going to touch you. Don't hit me."

He wraps his arms across your back and pulls you against him. It feels nothing like a hug. Instead, you're immobilized. It makes you think of someone calming an animal, or a kid who's been screaming. Too tight against your belly.

You twist, and he gives immediately. You wonder, suddenly, if he's afraid of you. Even when you just lean back against him, with your belly free, he pauses for a long time before he wraps his arms across your chest, just under your collarbone.

Up close, you can hear his lungs. His heart's not close enough to your ears, but his pulse thrusts against the skin of his forearms, and you can feel that.

Breathe. You realize how tired you are. You've been up for eighteen hours. It's three in the morning.

Chris says, "Amory, you gotta leave people alone."

"I see less than two people a day."

"You forget why we live out here? It's to be alone. If you didn't want to be, you shouldn't have come."

"I came here for my mom."

"Your mom would be okay. I check on her, and Ryan does. She fits into some important part of his psyche. And she reminds him to take his pills."

He walks you back to the bed. Lets go and crawls in and turns to face the wall.

You lie down with your feet at his head and stare at the ceiling. Get up again and turn off the lights.

"Why is Ryan on medication?"

"His business. He won't hurt you. He just. He worries about the animals. He's better since she moved back. You, not so much." Chris' voice is muffled, like he's very serious about going back to sleep.

You lie on your back and listen to him fall asleep. Later, when you're cold, you drag yourself up to the pillow so you can share the covers. You're in your running clothes, and Chris has his jeans on, and you could be sleeping over at age nine. It's windier, now, than when you let yourself in. The wind sounds less like water in Chris' house, though. You hear it pulling at the cheap aluminum siding. If you hold very still, it sounds like moving cars.

11.

Your mom stays online for hours, even in daylight. She's having low-speed chat conversations with someone, saving the logs religiously, and then printing them out on the yellowing fan-fold paper that she stole when she left work. They sit around the house, waiting for you to read them.

You're resisting. If she wants to tell you something, she can say it out loud.

Chris doesn't come by for breakfast for more than a week. He dropped you at the driveway's mouth on his way to work, the morning after you let yourself into his place, and didn't say anything.

You're bored. The thing is kicking. You ignore it.

Eventually, you start cleaning. There's a collection of ancient chemicals under the sink, and you exhaust those on the first day. Toilet-bowl blue, lemon-scented all-purpose cleaner, ancient bars of Sunlight soap that you rub against old, soaked towels to scrub down the walls. The blue fumes make you dizzy enough that you eventually go outside. Sit in the shade and listen to the bugs hum and watch Ryan moving ancient machines around his yard through the trees. Go back in and scrub another patch of ancient wallpaper.

When the cleaners are gone, you dig in the backs of cupboards for vinegar and baking soda. One quick binge of mixing them together in honour of your elementary school science experiments. You keep them separate afterwards, using the soda to take stains off and the vinegar to strip away smells. You open the fridge and let it defrost, melt everything into sludge. There isn't much left in it; you need to get groceries. If you could get to Saskatoon, you think, the dollar stores might have more vinegar. More rags.

You run out of cleaners.

You ask Ryan, first. Wait until he's in the yard, with a clear escape route, then come begging for cleansers. Anything he's got under the sink or in the closet. You'll replace it later. Promise.

"Oh. Sure, sorry. I should have cleaned it. Like, before your mom moved in."

"I'm pretty sure it was clean when she moved in. You have to keep doing it if you want a place to stay that way."

He nods. Goes into the house and comes out with grocery bags full of half-full bottles and a promise he'll get you more if you want it.

You take on the bathroom. The tub's enamel was stripped when you were a kid: some kind of abrasive ripped its smooth surface off and left it rough and vaguely grey-dirty. It's worse now. Soap scum, you think. One of those terms you've heard on TV all your life, never quite as vivid as it is under your nails. It doesn't come off with a cloth and lemon cleanser. It needs, you've decided, to come off. You have rubber gloves, now. You can take on anything. You just need to experiment.

Glass cleaner doesn't work. It makes brighter streaks in the mess, but doesn't remove it. It wasn't your best idea: you should have saved it for the windows.

The bleach you try next isn't your best idea either.

It's not a lot. You remember why you aren't supposed to mix those a few seconds after you've added bleach to water and soaked the tub with it. The bathroom window's open. It vents enough of the chlorine gas that you can flee the house.

Only, your mom is upstairs, possibly sleeping, and you're not sure she has any windows open at all.

218 • YOU ARE NOT NEEDED NOW

You think for a while about whether, if she died, they'd be able to tell how it happened. Where you might go, afterwards. Vancouver, maybe. You haven't really tried living on the west coast yet. It rains there all the time. For years when you were little, it didn't rain at all, and you always wanted it to. You might have to live on the coast for years before you get too waterlogged and have to leave.

You're not sure that kids who're born on the coast can survive anywhere else.

She's still asleep when you go up to check on her. The computer's dozing, eating energy even in its dormant state, so you wake it, risk the Internet howls, and ask it how much chlorine gas is toxic. The Internet informs you that chlorine sinks into low-lying areas.

Like a horror movie: don't go into the basement.

You lie down beside her on the mattress and think about the insides of your lungs. Drift.

Ryan comes looking for you. You wonder, later, how much he's been watching the house, to notice that you disappeared.

You aren't prepared for him in the bedroom. You're curled up with your mother. She woke up for a while and typed on the singing computer, went away and came back, and you got up when she was asleep and did the same things. It takes twenty minutes for a street map of Vancouver to load. You're thinking about where, maybe, you could afford to live. Checking out Craigslist for people who need housemates. Drift off and rouse to sever the connection. Sleep.

You only wake up when Ryan touches your neck. Fingers on your carotid, and it's horrible for long seconds while it doesn't occur to you that he might be taking your pulse. You can only stare at him. Eyes on the man in the bedroom bending over your body. His other hand's on the mattress, and he might not have meant to lean it on your breast, but there it is. He's too close.

The keyboard's in the bed, between you and your mom. When you hit Ryan with it, the cord rips away from the computer and the tower falls in a scream of off-kilter cooling fan.

12.

Chris takes you to the hospital with Ryan. He can't convince your mom to leave the house. He didn't — it occurs to you to be grateful for this — call the police.

Ryan needs stitches in his forehead. Chris tells them to check your lungs for poisoning. Just like he's been looking in your bathroom.

They tell him you're fine. Ask him if you have a delivery plan. If the two of you do.

Ryan's mother picks him up from the hospital. She looks awful. You realize you haven't seen her in twenty-three years, and that she's older than you remember her. She looks worse, though. Like she collects Ryan from Emergency a lot.

In the truck, driving home, Chris says, "Have you thought any more about leaving?"

"I'm looking for a place in Vancouver."

"Good idea."

He drops you in his yard. Says, "I'm going to check on your mom. Go to bed."

You wake up in the afternoon. Chris cleaned up around you, and left at some point, you think to go to work. He's back and showered and combing his hair in the bedroom mirror, you think watching you. He waits until you admit you're awake to say, "Get dressed."

"Why?"

"I want you to go into town with me."

He says this like he's planning to have you arrested, but in fact he takes you to church in Swanson, in mid-afternoon on a weekday. You don't realize fully until he's pulled into the gravel lot alongside. From the back, the place looks institutional. A hospital or a police block, nothing like the asymmetrical architectural monstrosity you remember haunting your childhood.

They still have the pamphlets, though. You recognize the ones on alienation, and suicide. A new one for depression looks suspiciously like the old one for Satanism.

Chris has seen some of your tattoos. Your dreadlocks are fully visible now. You're wearing May's belly-wrap, and you spent your nights haunting the organic-farming Christians of your neighbourhood until the geese rose up from hell to drive you out. You say, "You could've at least asked me to pray with you at home and saved yourself the gas."

"I'm not asking you to pray with me. I don't think you're in a conversion mood."

"Why, then?"

"Marilyn wants to talk to you about your mom. I thought it was probably a good idea."

In the church, he looks less like the Crystal you remember, or even the guy who's been hanging around your place, and more like the Christian you didn't trust by the side of the road. Weirdly masculine, like he learned to be a man by haunting the steps of cowboy Promise-Keepers.

When you were a teenager, living with your father, the Promise Keepers came for him. Your father's a sweet guy; he let them come in and talk. They told him how his marriage ended because he wasn't prepared to man up and take responsibility for his family. He *put too much on the shoulders of women*, is what you remember. Left them to make too many decisions. It fractured the family, because he wouldn't take his place.

We're telling you this because we fear for your daughters.

I only have one left at home.

The more reason. The others may be beyond your reach. This one you can help.

How?

Be her father. The patriarch she needs. Protect her. You can ask her now, ask her to commit her purity to you, put it in your keeping until you can help her choose a husband.

Have you ever seen my daughter?

It's why we came. We didn't want either of you to fall too far, to move again before we could reach out and help.

They left him with books and pamphlets and a catalogue for purity rings he could buy and use to bind you to him until your holy wedding. He sat there and looked at them until you got curious enough to come look at them too.

You said, "They think I'm a slut?"

"And they don't even know you're a witch. Imagine if they did."

His voice, saner than your mom's, is the one you call up when you need to walk away from people. He said things like that to you a couple more times before you understood he meant, *If they were smart, they'd be scared of you.*

Marilyn is a middle-aged lesbian pastor who looks enough like Bernie to pass for her at a distance. She was converted, she tells you, on the road to Sturgis, South Dakota. "I had to tell my girls I was plotting to bring down the church from within," she tells you. "I don't think they much cared which church. If they'd been thinking, they'd have realized it was one that takes lesbian pastors."

"Takes them where?"

"Well, not to the stake. I share office space here because the United Church building turned out to have asbestos in it."

You stare.

She says, "When these ones imagined the coming of the Lord, they didn't think the Pentecost was going to look like me. It's fun. And I do alright with the old people. Anyway." She hands you tea. It's herbal, no sugar. No tea bag. The leaves loose in the bottom look like they might have been gathered by the witches at your summer camp. She says, "You need to think about what's best for your mother."

This is, you realize, a conversational riptide. You're no longer where you thought you were standing.

"Chris called me. I called your sisters. I suspected they didn't realize how bad your mother's condition is. They were, at least, under the impression you were taking care of things."

"I am taking care of things. I even cleaned."

"You gassed yourself. And I gather you recently committed assault with ancient computer hardware."

"Jesus. Is this an *intervention?*"

"If it were, I'd have tried to assemble a few more people you know. Call it a friendly-advice ambush. Your mother stopped coming to church months ago. I gather it's about when you showed up. Are you uncomfortable with Christianity?"

"I'm uncomfortable with Christians. Like Gandhi. I don't know what you're up to."

"The Mahatma may have had a point. You don't. No one is trying to hunt or harm you. But your mother accommodates you, and she wouldn't want to provoke the kind of confrontation that her church-going might spark. Then she stopped buying groceries. Then she stopped leaving the house."

Pastor Marilyn glares at you. "You're not *helping* her, Amory. Possibly you're helping yourself, but it's parasitic.

"You need to leave."

You stare at her.

"If you can erase the fiction that you're caring for her, she will have to get help, or commit to caring for herself."

"She'll starve."

"She can drive. I expect she'll go grocery shopping once she has to."

"She doesn't get out of bed."

"You make sure she doesn't have to."

You think about this. Look from Marilyn to Chris. "Which one of you decided I should leave?"

"I don't think that's relevant. I'd suggest you stay with Chris for a few days while you think about what to do. In any case, you're shortly not going to be in any position to care for a mentally ill parent. Presuming you're planning to keep it."

You get up. "Fuck you both. Good trick getting me here. I don't have any way home. But I'm not going back with *that*." Pointing at Chris.

Marilyn says, "Except your mother's house, I can give you a ride to wherever you need to go."

13.

Ryan is afraid of you. He ducks around corners when you emerge from the bedroom, and he leaves the house when you come downstairs. His meds are lined up neatly by the sink. You wonder, if you just sat here for days, would he come past you to take them, or would he sit outside and go quietly mad?

You can't think of anything that would have irritated Chris more. Ryan's afraid of you, but he came and carried your stuff from your mom's house to his, and cleared an extra space that you remember being his brother's room just to put the flattened nursery furniture all in one place.

You grinned at him. Poured kitchen salt across the threshold, to see if he'd cross it voluntarily.

If he has, he hasn't broken the line. He's busy with harvest, and moving animals, and his bedroom's on the main floor, so arguably, he has a reason not to be near you. You'd just like to know why he took you in.

Too many witches in one place.

Chris has stolen your mom. He came over, pushing past you, and went upstairs to visit her. Kept talking until she got dressed and came downstairs. You couldn't quite remember when she'd last done that. But they talked, and you left the house, and when you came back Chris and your mom had packed a couple of old nylon gym bags with her favourite things, and he had her computer in pieces, and they left. Went back to his place. When you jogged by, later, she was outside, feeding his chickens, like a person who had a normal relationship with daylight.

What Chris told Ryan you have no idea, but Ryan came for you.

So the house is empty. Your mother's a middle-aged, hippy-dyke-looking woman housekeeping for a boy-girl thing who pulls for Jesus, and you live with the mental patient next door.

He won't fuck you.

He's beautiful. Whatever your friend saw in him when you were kids is gone, but Ryan turned into the kind of solidly male body that you love. His clothes, piled by the washing machine in the basement, smell male enough that you spend time down there with them, sticky-fingered, and then do the laundry because otherwise his T-shirt will glare under black light.

There is no Internet in Ryan's house. No electronics at all, in fact. No TV. No microwave. There's one small tape player, and a box of nearly worn-out tapes from the 80s and 90s, and another box containing a tangle of plug-adaptors that don't seem to belong to anything. There are only a couple of lamps, and no bulbs in the overhead sockets.

He has enough candles to fuel your adolescent fantasies of medieval life.

You spend your nights reading May's pregnancy books. After a week, you strip naked and start measuring the changes in your hips. If you'd studied this sooner, you could have used a mirror to track the state of your cervix. With the right camera attachment, you could have documented it and installed the film somewhere vividly chaste as an art project.

Several small pamphlets May included involve pro-and-con lists on the subject of eating the placenta.

You could feed it to Ryan. He probably thinks you're already planning to.

Outside, it's brutally dark. There are cattle on two sides of the small yard. The hogs in the distance reek: their sterile environment doesn't extend to the neutralization of the liquid pig-shit they're spreading over the neighbouring fields. Your mother's feeding chickens, and maybe cows by now. The cultists down the road have hogs and geese.

All these animals and not one sacrifice to scare the children.

The house you left behind is locked. You have to break a panel-window in the door to let yourself in. It's dark in there, and the fridge is propped open because the power is off. Without occupants, without power, you wonder how long it'll stand. The house wasn't in good shape even when you arrived, and now the basement's tangled up with mustard gas and the corners are sticky with your memories of pre-pubescent sexual curiosity and adult perversion.

If you were better prepared, you could at least set fire to it. You didn't bring anything.

Tomorrow.

You go back out and lie down in the grass to picture it. Mentally pack a bag. Leave in the night. If you leave your mom a post-dated cheque for her car, you could take that. You have enough cash to make it to Saskatoon, at least. If some place needs a vegan cook, you can make yourself useful, make a couple of bucks, and leave the debate on placental cookery for your next life.

You have to remember to bring matches. Maybe gasoline. Fire consumes everything. It means you have to start over. It's more fun every time it happens.

Clean Streets Are Everyone's Responsibility

THE CITY ISSUED A MEMO EARLY IN THE SNOWMELT making bus drivers responsible for the collection of hands. They didn't bother to print it on official letterhead. Just mailed it out to the supervisors and had them shove a print-out into everyone's locker, so that the pages fell on us when we got to work. It was a good trick. If they'd given us any warning, we could have lodged a complaint. Something about biohazards or inappropriate working conditions. Instead, the memo reached us about the same time that the announcement went out on the morning news.

In response to the large number of hands which have been discovered in melting snow drifts, the city has established an interim hand-collection policy. Winnipeg residents are encouraged to wrap any discovered hands appropriately (in grocery bags, etc.) and turn them in to city bus drivers. Drivers will return all hands to a central collection point, from which the city will make all reasonable efforts to ascertain the hands' origins and identify their owners. If you are unable to wait for the next bus, please leave the hand at your nearest bus stop. Ensure the wrapping is labelled clearly.

I was braced for ugly, wet bags waiting in piles at otherwise empty bus stops, stinking and slowing down the route, but in fact most people waited in person to submit their discoveries. I was issued a big plastic box, red and yellow, to hold the results. There were very few grocery bags. Instead, I carefully accepted bundles wrapped in old baby blankets and sweaters. There were a couple that at first I thought might be kittens, or something else little and still alive. It meant I had to check. Pull back the wrapping and ensure that whatever I'd been given wasn't going to suffocate. They were all hands. People took it very seriously.

The snowmelt always reveals a few ugly things that stayed politely frozen all winter. There's the layer of dog shit and garbage and small animals that didn't survive. The police force is in my union, for some reason, and they told us that bodies turn up every spring, dead all winter and picked at by scavengers, and suddenly everyone's very urgent about it, just like the poor guys weren't missing all winter.

The first few hands were collected by the police with full forensic teams. The city was worried, the way they were in Vancouver when feet started washing up on the beach. People started talking about serial killers.

Later, when they started to desensitize, people made jokes about secret implementations of Sharia law. Even before the hand-collection program started, at the bus sheds we received a couple of reminders that anti-Muslim sentiment wasn't welcome in the department. That all residents of the city who gave respect deserved to receive respect. It was phrased like that, about giving and receiving respect, because of the crazies, and the right we'd won in the last strike to eject them if they started to get rowdy. We got our safety shields in that strike, too. Taxi drivers only got safety shields this year.

Because of the shield, I had to climb down every time someone gave me a hand. It didn't seem right to just say, *Put it in the box with the others.* I had to come out and accept the wrapped-up thing, and tell the waiting person *Thanks.* Like it was a lost iPod or something: *You did the right thing. I'll make sure it gets back to its owner.*

The police relaxed when they got a sense of how many hands were actually out there. It seems counterintuitive that they'd breathe easier when the number passed a thousand, but it was evidence that the hands couldn't possibly have been severed from city residents. People would have noticed. The hands were only hands, not evidence of bodies. They were neatly severed just above all those tiny wrist bones, with no extra osteotic fragments. It was done really neatly. And because they were mostly still frozen, the hands didn't really smell. There were some white hands and some brown hands and some black hands, men's hands and women's hands. No children's hands. That helped. I don't think I could have just accepted a child's hand from some stranger hunched over waiting at Keewatin and Inkster.

The second week of collection, I lined my box with a flannel sheet from the top of my closet. The police sent us notes about the status of the hands. The notes went up on the bulletin board next to our lockers. When they determined that nearly all the hands were lefts, they told us. Later, they added that about one in seven were right hands. They were all dead, obviously, but it wasn't immediately clear whether they'd been severed before or after death. The medical examiner wasn't even really sure how the hands had been severed, since there were no broken bones, and the cut ends were so even.

They were just hands. There weren't anywhere near six hundred thousand, though I kept hearing people on the bus speculating that maybe there was an extra hand for every person in the city. Still, the police cadets were pressed into service fingerprinting them all. Students from both universities came in to take DNA samples. The city petitioned the province for funds to catalogue and preserve the hands until they could be properly something-ed. The regional health authority invited people to come in and submit DNA samples, just in case.

That triggered the poster campaign. I was working a north end route, so I mostly didn't see the signs until I took a few days off. The posters went up in the city core and the hipster villages south of the Assiniboine River. The kind of areas you can travel on foot, or on a skateboard. I tried not to read anything into that. Not everybody rides the bus, not by a long shot. I see the odd bumper sticker, while I'm stuck in traffic, that reads, *Anyone caught on a bus after 30 has failed at life.*

A few whack jobs are banned from transit. We have pictures of them up on the bulletin board, just in case, though most of them only ever haunted a couple of routes, and didn't try to crash new ones.

The campaign posters were hand-drawn and photocopied. They warned us all against submitting DNA samples. The police, they said, were just trying to make a catalogue of all citizens. Below that it said, *Smash the state! Learn to skate!* We tried not to take that as a slam against the transit system, either.

The hands dwindled once the snow was gone. The odd one was discovered in Assiniboine Forest, chewed by dogs or coyotes, and a couple washed up on the river banks, but they were obvious leftovers. No new ones appeared.

The city didn't identify any of the hands right away, or later on, either.

There wasn't actually a one-to-one ratio of hands to city residents; more like one-to-one-hundred. The final tally of hands was 6,841. They're carefully wrapped and stored in the Health Sciences Centre, now. All in little bags, with tags indicating what they were wrapped in when they arrived, and details like nail polish colour. I found out that last detail when I signed up for a tour. They have a little fact sheet they give out to the curious. It lists the number of men's hands and women's, and how many there were by race, roughly, and odd little things like the fact that while lots had tan shadows, three actually had wedding rings on. Seven had tattoos.

If they can't trace the hands within ten years, the official plan is to release them in bunches to religious groups, so they can hold funerals. It'll be proportionate. Nobody has a plan for the atheist hands. It'll probably depend on how religious the city council is feeling at the time, whether they leave room for atheists.

I keep hearing a rumour, though, through the union newsletter and work chatter, that if the religious thing falls through, they're going to give the hands up for adoption. Sort of like kittens. So I put my name in for that. I'll take in a hand. Maybe bury it in my flower bed. I carried so many of them, I feel like I owe them something.

ABOUT THE AUTHOR

Annette Lapointe was born on the coldest day of 1978, in Saskatoon, which might explain her ongoing affinity for the prairies. She has lived in rural Saskatchewan, Quebec City, St. John's, Winnipeg, and Seoul and Jinju in South Korea, before migrating to Grande Prairie, Alberta, where it's cold most of the time but the wildlife comes right up to the door and asks to come in.

Her first novel, *Stolen* (2006), was nominated for a Giller Prize and was the winner of two Saskatchewan Book Awards (First Book Award and Saskatoon Book Award). A finalist for the Books in Canada First Novel Award, as well as being cited as a *Globe & Mail* Top 5 First Fiction choice, *Stolen* also garnered Lapointe a Canadian Authors Association-BookTV Emerging Writer award. Her second novel, *Whitetail Shooting Gallery* (2012), was a finalist for the McNally Robinson Book of the Year.

Lapointe completed her PhD in Contemporary Literature in 2010. She now teaches at Grande Prairie Regional College and edits *The Waggle* magazine.